MAMA DEE

MAMA DEE

EARL LYNN

Charleston, SC
www.PalmettoPublishing.com

Mama Dee

First Edition

Paperback ISBN: 978-1-64990-898-8
eBook ISBN: 978-1-63837-714-6

In Loving Memory of Sandy
and Annie Laura Strickland

CONTENTS

CHAPTER 1

The Homecoming

Spring 1942—As hard rain falls on this foggy moonlit night, an intoxicated driver makes his way down the curvy wet road near the levee. He wipes his windshield with his handkerchief as he struggles to make out the words on a sign that someone has hand-painted and placed on the side of the road. While trying to read the sign, the front tire of his car runs over something in the middle of the road, causing it to rattle and swerve. He quickly directs his attention back to the road as best he can.

After traveling a bit farther, the car starts to wobble.

"Damn! A flat tire," he mumbles to himself as he pulls over to the side of the road. After waiting a while, hoping that the rain would slow down or maybe even stop, he decides to go ahead and change the tire in the rain. After getting out of the car, he makes his way to the trunk. The wind intensifies and starts to blow the rain in an almost horizontal direction; he places the jack underneath the car. It is now untenable for him to keep any part of his body from getting soaking wet.

While mumbling words of profanity, he continues to jack the car up into the air. After completing the tasks of jacking the car, he removes the flat tire and goes back around to the trunk to retrieve the spare tire from its mount. After lifting the spare onto the spindle, he holds it in place with one hand while trying to wipe the falling rain from his face with the sleeve of the other. But by this time, his jacket is soaking wet, and all he does is put more water into his eyes.

While still holding the spare tire on the spindle, he feels around on the ground for the lugs that he had taken off earlier when he removed the flat tire. But they are nowhere to be found.

"Where in the hell did I put the damn things?" he asks himself in a slurred dialogue while continuing to search around on the ground.

After not finding the lugs where he thought that he had put them, he stands and starts to walk back to the rear of the car but gets distracted as the spare tire falls from the spindle. While bending down to pick up the tire, he sees a patch of brush on the side of the road move as if there is something in it.

As the brush parts, something that looks like a white ball wobbles out of them and makes its way onto the road. At first, the object looks as if it were being controlled by the wind. But after a moment or so of watching it, he realizes that it is not for the wind is gusty and intermittently blowing in all directions. But the object is continuously moving in only one. As his curiosity about the unidentifiable object crossing the dark wet road deepens, it further distracts him from the task of changing the flat tire.

The drunken soul rubs his face once more as he again tries to remove the falling rainwater from his eyes. After making its way to the center of the road, about thirty feet in front of his car, the object stops.

He reaches into the car and turns on the headlights. What first looked to be a white ball rolling across the road is revealed by the beam of light from the lamps of the vehicle to actually be an albino opossum.

The man laughs as he staggers out onto the road to take a closer look at the strange-looking animal. As he walks up to it, the frightened creature rolls over onto its back and plays dead. It is then that he realizes that he has been so busy looking at the creature that he hasn't taken the time to look up or down the road since he followed the freak of nature out onto it.

And as his head rises, so does the volume of the shrieking sound coming from the tires of the oncoming speeding car as they are trying to cling to the wet pavement of the curve in the road. It is too late! Seconds later, his broken body lay in the ditch, trembling while the last fractured bits of life leave it.

The car comes to a stop thirty yards or so down the road past where his car is sitting. And it sits there for a moment as if the driver is contemplating what to do next. After the driver completes whatever thought process is needed to react to what had just happened, the car accelerates and speeds off into the night. After the car's taillights have vanished into the dark, the cunning oddity of nature returns to its feet and continue on its way.

* * *

Summer 1990—As Clarice turns onto the wet gravel road, Mama Dee sits quietly on the back seat and gazes out the automobile's window. She watches the sky as the gloomy gray clouds slowly roll across. The car rocks from side to side as its tires splash through the shallow water-filled potholes as the rain continues drizzling and seems to not want to let up. Mama Dee then starts to hum in a low and serene voice.

"What are you singing, Mama?" Clarice asks.

"Oh, nothing," answers Mama Dee as she continues to hum.

The gloomy, overcast sky and the drizzling rain seem to somehow add to the aura that Mama Dee carries within her heart about where they are now. And as the car passes the row of old rundown shacks, a tear slowly creeps from the corner of her eye and slowly makes its way down her cheek.

This was not only the place where Mama Dee was born and had lived well into her young adult life. It was also the place where her parents and grandparents were born, lived, and had died. And as the car turns onto the stretch of road that leads up to the main house, Mama Dee looks back over her shoulder at the vast open land that was once covered with rows and rows of cotton plants.

Once the car makes it to the top of the hill, Mama Dee looks out over her other shoulder at what remains of the once brightly whitewashed shacks that had housed the sharecroppers and their families for decades. She sees that time has not only aged her, but it has aged this place as well.

Other than the tiny collapsing shacks, there are only small bits and pieces of earthly things still remaining. And although time has tried to erase what it could of this place, it hasn't expunged or aged the memories of it in the least. And as the memories start to slowly unwind in Mama Dee's mind, it is as if time is taking her back to then.

Even though there is little about the place that looks the same, all Mama Dee has to do is close her eyes and feel the wind as it caresses her face or taste the air as it enters her lungs to know where she is and be reminded of the events that took place here.

These memories are far beyond being engraved in her mind; they are etched in her very soul and are a big part of what she has evolved into. And all at once, both the good and the bad memories start to rise up from deep within the crevices of her mind and into the forefront of her present day.

Clarice holds an umbrella as she assists Mama Dee in getting out of the car. Once out of the car, Mama Dee stands in front of the rustic old mansion with its covered wraparound porch. She stares down into the valley once more at the forgotten remnants of the little shacks that dot the hillsides and the valley below.

"Mama Dee, why don't you sit here on the porch while I try and find the keys to the front door?" Clarice says as she heads back to the car.

Mama Dee sits down on the bench next to the front door and then looks out at a distant bluff where the cotton gin used to be. Her mind then drifts back to a time and day when she was simply known as DeEtta. And while her mind is there, the events of that day begin to replay themselves.

* * *

Fall 1928—DeEtta is eight years old, and the days are hard and long as the cotton-picking season end nears.

"*Holy cow*! That boy can pick some cotton!" JJ shouts out while looking at the scale that has Nathan's sack of cotton hanging from it.

"Aw, shut up, JJ!" Steven replies as he reaches into his pocket and flips his brother a nickel.

"I think this is the fourth time that I've won this week! You keep losing like this, Poppa is going to have to give you one of those cotton sacks!" JJ says as he laughs and maneuvers himself so that he keeps outside of his brother's reach. "*Isn't that right, Pa!*" he shouts as he runs through the crowd of sharecroppers standing in front of the counter.

"*Y'all boys take that outside now!*" Big John yells out. He then looks back over at Nathan and says, "Nathan, if you and that boy of yours keep picking like that, you might be able to break even in the next couple of picking seasons." As a couple of Big Johns white friends who happened to be in the warehouse at the time, burst out into laughter. Big John, slightly smiles as he writes something down in his logbook and tells Nathan to make his mark next to it.

As Nathan makes his mark, his son Jimmy Lee is standing next to him. Jimmy Lee stares down at the numbers on the paper but is quickly brushed aside when the white man standing behind the counter yells out, "Next!" At the time, Jimmy Lee is just fourteen years old and can pick over a hundred and fifty pounds of cotton a day.

DeEtta, her brother Sandy Earl, and her father Sonny watch silently while standing next to their sacks of cotton. JJ and Steven run past them and out the door. JJ then turns and sticks his head back inside and asks, "Sandy Earl, Jimmy Lee! Do y'all want to come fishing with us?" He then lets out a heckle.

But before either Sandy Earl or Jimmy Lee can answer, Big John yells out, *"I thought I told y'all to get y'all's asses out of here now!"*

JJ quickly retreats back out the door, knowing that Sandy Earl and Jimmy Lee had better not answer yes in front of Big John or their fathers.

As JJ and his brother take off racing down the road toward the creek, Sandy Earl looks over at his father, Sonny, hoping for some instruction on what to do next. Sonny looks over at Sandy Earl and slightly tilts his head, signaling to Sandy Earl to keep quiet. Jimmy Lee looks down toward the ground as Nathan quickly takes him by the arm and walks out the door.

Although Jimmy Lee had not uttered a word, Sandy Earl knew that he was in trouble because JJ had asked them to come fishing in front of the entire room. And everyone there could tell that it had embarrassed Big John in front of his white friends and workers standing behind the counter and up on the scale platform. And the saddest thing of all was that the only crime that Jimmy Lee had committed that day was being asked to come fishing.

Sonny and Sandy Earl's sacks of cotton is then lifted onto the scale to be weighed. After their sacks of cotton are weighed, Big John looks for Sonny's name in his book. "Mm...I see that your rent and store account is all paid up," he says as he rubs his hand across the grayish whiskers on his face.

"How many kids do you and Mary have now?" Big John asks.

"Two, sir! Sandy Earl and our girl DeEtta," Sonny replies as he points in their direction.

"I got the boys building some new shacks along the road down there. And I'm wondering if you and Mary would like to move into one of them. I'll bet it's almost twice as much room as y'all have now. What do you think?" Big John asks. "It'll only be a few dollars more for rent," he adds.

As Sonny listens to what Big John is offering, several thoughts circulate around in his head. The first is the sight of his two children sleeping on the floor every night. The second is how cold it gets in the wintertime when the wind blows in through the openings around the windows and doors and sometimes up through the cracks in the floors of the house that they now live in. But his main thoughts are how Big John will react if he declines his offer.

After Big John finishes his spiel, Sonny replies, "I surely would appreciate that, Mr. Shegogg."

Big John puts his hand on Sonny's shoulder as they walk together toward the door and adds, "Now, I want you and Mary to go down to the store and pick out some new furniture for y'all new house, you hear. And I won't take no for an answer."

As Sonny, DeEtta, and Sandy Earl walk home that night, Sonny feels good because he knows that his children will no longer need to sleep on the floor. But he also feels some sadness because he and Mary want a place of their own so badly. And spending the extra money will only push them farther away from accomplishing that dream.

When they get home that evening, Sonny walks in the house with a big smile on his face. "How is my lovely wife doing this evening?" he asks.

Mary knows right away that something is afoot. "Out of all the days that I have known you, it's only been twice that I have seen you come home from the fields happy. The first time was when Mr. Shegogg's brother Jeffery fell off of his horse and killed himself while trying to hit Bo with the mule strap. And the other was when I brought your dinner out to the field, and nine months later, we had DeEtta. So…what is going on? And what did you do?" Mary asks.

"I had a conversation with Mr. Shegogg about us getting a bigger place. I know that it's going to cost more and that will cut into how much we can put away every season for a place of our own. But, Mary, our children are sleeping on the floor, and we practically freeze to death every winter," Sonny says. And before Mary can respond, he adds, "And he said that we can go down to the store and pick out some new furniture too."

Mary exhales and says, "Do you remember how long it took for us to get out of his debt when we got this place that we now live in? As far as them Shegoggs are concerned, slavery never ended. They just changed the name to sharecropping."

They all then sit down at the table, Sonny blesses the meal that Mary has prepared, and they eat their dinner.

CHAPTER 2

Paid in Full

S ummer 1990—"What are you thinking about, Mama Dee?" Clarice asks as she searches through a ring of keys for the key to the front door.

"Nothing much, honey," Mama Dee replies.

After finding the key, Clarice opens the front door, looks over at Mama Dee, and says, "Stefan and the kids will be here tomorrow. That should not only lift your spirits, but it will also give you somebody to yell at!"

Mama Dee smiles and replies, "You know I don't yell anymore…that much."

As Clarice laughs, she says, "Why don't you come on in with me so that you can see what the designer has done with the house. I'm sure you're going to love it."

Mama Dee slowly rises to her feet and walks into the foyer. The house has been redone down to the sprawling oak staircase that leads up to the multiple bedroom suites. Mama Dee looks at the towering staircase and says, "You're right, this sure is beautiful. But I hope you're not planning on me walking up and down all those steps every day. Because if you are, I'll be in the car waiting on a ride back to my house."

Clarice laughs again and says, "No! We do not want you to walk up or down the stairs, Mama Dee. We had an elevator installed! Come on back to the kitchen, and I'll show it to you." After riding the elevator up to the second level, Clarice shows Mama Dee to her room.

After looking at the room, Mama Dee says to Clarice, "There was a time when our whole family lived in a house smaller than this room."

Clarice says, "Yes, I know. Jamil and Jazmin have told me practically each and every story that you have ever told them about your childhood and how hard you had it growing up."

Mama Dee follows Clarice into the master bedroom suite. The suite has tall ceilings with expensive-looking ceiling fans hanging from them. The entry doors and French doors leading to the balcony are all eight-foot-tall with fancy carvings.

Clarice opens the doors leading to the balcony and walks out. "Come on out, Mama Dee, you have just got to see this view," Clarice says as she walks over to the railing and gazes at the seemingly endless view.

Mama Dee walks out onto the balcony and looks out over the countryside. She then walks over to one of the large wicker chairs and sits down. Continuing to look out, she says, "You know, I lived on this place until I was in my twenties and never once saw it from this view. Now I see why Ms. Shegogg liked to sit and look out from up here. She could see everything. And from here, everything looks so peaceful."

"Why don't you sit here and enjoy the view while I go and fix you a glass of lemonade and me something a little stronger?" Clarice says as she walks back into the house. While Mama Dee is sitting there, a large crow lands on the railing and starts to squawk at her. She shoos him off by waving one of the pillows from the wicker chair at him.

She watches the crow as it flies high into the sky and then comes back down and lands in a rather large willow tree that is sitting next to a now overgrown road. The sight and location of the willow tree makes Mama Dee start to tremble. *Could that be the same tree?* she thinks. Her mind once again takes her back to a time.

* * *

Fall 1929—"DeEtta! You need to keep up if we going to get there before dark," Mary says as she takes some cotton from DeEtta's sack and stuffs it into her own.

"Okay, Mama," DeEtta replies.

"We can't be late getting to the gin because Mr. Shegogg will be angry at us," Mary says as she picks up their pace while dragging the long sack filled with cotton behind her.

Mary and DeEtta arrive just in time for the start of the weigh-in. Mary drags in the heavy sack of cotton and places it next to her husband Sonny and her son Sandy Earl's four other sacks. DeEtta lays her small sack on top of them.

"Bring yours on over here, Sonny, you are next!" the white man behind the counter yells out.

"Y'all sure picked some cotton today!" Mr. Shegogg says as the last sack is placed onto the hook of the scale.

After looking at the reading on the scale, he writes something down in his book. And without allowing Sonny to read what he has written down, he tells him to put his mark next to it.

Mr. Shegogg is often referred to as Big John by most of his friends and the white folks around town with money or political influence. He owns the plantation where the cotton is grown, the gin where it is processed, the houses that most of the sharecroppers live in, and the only store within a thirty-mile radius. Some say that he has so much money, that he even owns the town's mayor and the sheriff department. His family originally lived in Louisiana where they had been slave owners for as far back as anyone can trace. Sometime before the Civil War, they picked up and moved to Mississippi where a great deal of them fought and died defending the aforementioned cause.

Sonny asks Big John, "Sir, would it be all right if I see what we picked today?" After looking at what Big John has written down in the book, Sonny says in a trembling voice, "Excuse me, Mr. Shegogg, I might be wrong…but I think that there should be a total of seven hundred pounds instead of four hundred on that addition. Sir?" A sudden hush falls over the room as Big John looks up from the book and into Sonny's eyes.

Big John's son Steven, who is in the sixth grade, is standing next to his dad. And before Big John can say anything, Steven says out loud, "He's right, Pop, you added it up wrong."

Big John quickly looks over at his son and then back at Sonny. Big John then says while giving Sonny one of the coldest stares one human could give another, "Maybe you're right, Sonny, I did make a mistake." Sonny knows that he has not only corrected one of the most powerful white men in Tallahatchie county, but he has done so in front of other white men who are deemed well beneath him and in front of other sharecroppers, who, as far as Big John is concerned, only exist to work his fields and clean his house.

After looking back down at the book, Big John adds, "I guess that makes your store credit balance paid in full for the season." He then points down at the book, indicating where Sonny needs to place his mark. Sonny picks up the pen and signs his name.

After seeing Sonny sign his name, one of the white workers behind the counter yells out, "I keep forgetting that this coon can sign his name!"

As the other white workers erupt into laughter, Sonny nods his head and whispers, "Thank you" to Big John.

Sonny and his family then head for home. As they walk down the dark road, DeEtta looks up at the star-lit night sky and asks her mother, "Mama, do the stars ever sleep?" But before her mother can answer, they hear the sounds of several horses trotting up the road behind them .

Sonny tells Mary to take the children and hide in the thickets off the road.

"Aren't you coming too?" Mary asks.

"No…honey, I got to face them. Because we can't run. Everything we got in this world is either on our backs or in that little house that we live in. And we got no place to run to. And besides, with the Depression being like it is, we'll all starve to death before winter. Now do like I tell you now. Go'n!"

As Mary and the children step off into the deep brush, she tells them to keep quiet as they squat down behind a large honeysuckle brush. The trotting sound ceases as the horses stop near the place where they left Sonny standing.

Mary covers DeEtta's ears as the sounds from the horses whining and her father screaming slice through the once silent night air. And only after what seems like forever has passed does a still silence once more reclaim the night. As she sniffles with grief, Mary tells DeEtta to stay put as she and Sandy Earl venture out to see what remains of her husband.

But as they move in the direction of Sonny, DeEtta follows close behind. And as they peek through the thickets at the road, they see Sonny's badly beaten and broken body lying on the ground under a small willow tree that sits next to the roadway. Mary, Sandy Earl, and DeEtta run over to his side.

"Sandy! You and DeEtta! Run as fast as you can to Mr. Bo's house. Tell him to come in a hurry and bring his wagon. And stay off the road!"

As DeEtta and her brother run as fast as their feet can take them into the night to get help, DeEtta knows that until the time comes for her to be laid to rest in her grave, each and every time she watches a star twinkle in the night sky, she will be reminded of this night.

CHAPTER 3

Not My Home

S ummer 1990—After dinner, Mama Dee goes up to her room while Clarice washes the dishes and puts away the remaining food. Once Clarice is done in the kitchen, she goes upstairs and checks on Mama Dee.

"How are you doing, Mama?" Clarice asks.

Mama Dee grunts and sits down in the rocking chair next to the window. She then starts to hum a song as she rocks back and forth in the chair.

Sensing that something is bothering her and she doesn't want to talk about it, Clarice picks another topic for conversation by saying, "Stefan and I got that rocking chair just for you. We both knew how much you like sitting and looking out at the birds and the flowers at your house back in Detroit."

Mama Dee replies, "Thanks" in a low and somewhat melancholy voice. She then turns and looks out the window at the large pines that now cover hillsides that were once speckled with the shacks of sharecroppers. She can now also better see what remains of the row of houses that once sat along the now overgrown road that once led to the meticulously chopped cotton fields that had, in years past, carpeted the valley below.

The once always freshly painted letters that adorned the tops of the row of tiny houses are now faded and worn. But the sight of their remnants strikes every nerve in Mama Dee's body as she looks upon what remains of the wooden shells that once brandished huge bright white letters upon their rooftops.

Although one can only now see the shaded outline of what was once so proudly displayed for the world to see and the Negroes of the field to fear as if their very existence depended on it, now it exists only as a memory. But what it represented at that time in her life is still etched in her memory as if it was just yesterday.

For she recalls, *"If any Negro who dared to be heard speaking untrue or marginally disrespectfully in reference to it, life was not only altered but, in some instances, snuffed out completely. And with less empathy than that given to a farm animal being butchered for feed for the dogs if the aforementioned monarch who answered to the surname chose to make it so."*

After seeing the row of houses, Mama Dee sits back in the chair and recalls when the letters were first painted on their rooftops.

* * *

1932—"DeEtta! Get in here and quit watching those boys! They have work to do!" Mary yells out while standing on the front porch.

"Coming, Mama!" DeEtta yells back. But before leaving, she gives her friend Julia Ann a note and tells her, "Give this to Marcus for me."

After taking the note, they giggle as DeEtta runs toward home like her Mama told her to do. Julia Ann walks over toward the house where Marcus is working. Marcus is standing on top of the roof with a paintbrush in his hand.

'What are you doing, Marcus?" Julia Ann asks while looking up at him from the ground.

"What does it look like I'm doing? I'm painting!" he sarcastically replies.

"I got something here for you from a special friend," Julia Ann says as she puts the note on top of the bucket of paint that is sitting next to the ladder. She then puts a rock on top of it so that it doesn't blow away.

"So who is this special friend?" Marcus asks as he stops what he is doing and walks over to the edge of the roof.

"That's for me to know and for you to find out," Julia Ann replies.

No sooner does Julia Ann get her reply out of her mouth, when John Shegogg Jr walks up. He and his brother Steven have been watching Marcus and Julia Ann talk from up the road.

"Hi, Julia Ann," John Jr. says as he looks her up and down.

Julia Ann looks down at the ground and replies, "Good morning, Mr. JJ."

John Jr. then turns his attention to Marcus, who is still up on the roof and has now started back to painting.

"You need to be paying attention to what you're doing up there, boy. Instead of flirting with these girls down here," John Jr. says.

Marcus replies with a feeble, "Yes, sir, JJ," as he continues to look down at what he is painting.

Julia Ann turns and walks off while John Jr. is talking to Marcus. Steven then walks up and says to John Jr., "Why are you messing with them, JJ? Come on, let's go."

After watching Julia Ann walk off, John Jr. picks up the note from under the rock and reads it. He then says, "So…I see that DeEtta is sweet on you. Um…" And then he balls the note up and sticks it in his pocket. As he walks away, he yells out, "And, boy! Don't fuck up the spelling of our last name!"

The next morning, the whole place is talking about what Mr. Shegogg had Marcus and a couple of the other boys paint on top of the row of shacks along the road. Ms. Lillie is the Black woman who cleans the Shegogg's house, and she saw it first thing that morning while washing their upstairs windows.

"There it was, as big as life, the word *Shegogg* in large white letters. I bet you that they can be seen from an airplane," Ms. Lillie tells Mary while they are sitting on the front porch of Mary's house shelling peas.

"I guess now everybody will be saying that you live in the G1 house, being that you live in the house with the first big G on top of it. And the other G houses will be called the G2 and G3 houses," Ms. Lillie concludes.

Mary just grunts and doesn't say anything.

That night, when Sonny gets home from the fields, Mary knows what will be on his mind. So she makes his favorite meal, a big pot of crowder peas and a large skillet of crackling cornbread. After dinner, Mary and Sonny go out on the front porch to talk.

"How much money do we have saved up now?" Sonny asks.

"Right at three hundred dollars," Mary answers.

"I know Mr. Monroe said that he wanted four hundred and fifty dollars for that land. But I am going to go and see him tomorrow. And I will beg him to let us have it for this here three hundred dollars if I got to. We will pay the rest as we get it. Mary! I'll be damned if I live in this house with that bastard's name on it after what they did to me." Sonny says as he wipes the tears of anger from his face.

DeEtta and Sandy Earl had sneaked over next to the door so that they could listen to what their parents are talking about. After finishing the conversation with Mary, Sonny gets up and limps back into the house. DeEtta and Sandy Earl both scramble away from the door and pretend as if they haven't heard a word.

The next day, Sandy and DeEtta are both happy and sad, happy because they know that they will perhaps get a place of their own and sad because they will be leaving their friends and everyone that they have ever known behind.

They had come to see the other sharecroppers as family, especially those who lived and grew up on the place with them. They had all attended the same one-room school together, attended the same church, and even got their water from the same well. Some of the women even did their laundry together and shared gardens. They both know that it will be tough for them to sever the ties.

The only other living relatives that DeEtta and Sandy Earl know about had moved up north and off to California when they were little kids and had not been heard from or seen since. As far as DeEtta and Sandy Earl know, they all could be dead.

The following day is Sunday. On Sundays, pretty much all of the Negroes in and around the area attend the Sunny Mount Baptist Church. The church is located just off the road on the other side of the creek, just past the bridge. The church is not only a place to recharge your faith. It serves as a place where the field workers could catch up on what was going on in each other's respective parts of the world, which, in some cases, meant catching up on the latest gossip.

"Honey! You wouldn't believe what Mr. Shegogg had painted on top of the new living quarters he had built," Ms. Lillie says to the lady who is sitting next to her as the preacher starts the sermon.

"Lord, what did he do this time?" the lady asks.

Ms. Lillie looks over her shoulder and sees DeEtta, Sara, and Julia Ann sitting behind them. She then whispers, "He painted his name as big as day across the tops of them. And after he did what he done to Sonny."

Knowing that Sonny and his family live in one of the once coveted homes and what he had done to Sonny, the lady replies, "I would burn it down before I lived in it!"

DeEtta, Sara, and Julia Ann pretend as if they are not paying attention to what Ms. Lillie and the lady are talking about. But still, they hear, and Sara and Julia Ann know that it had hurt DeEtta's feelings even though she is trying her best to hide it.

And as Reverend Mitchel intensifies in his sermon, Ms. Lillie and the lady continue to gossip. And without warning, something happens that DeEtta and Sara thought that they would never ever witness: Julia Ann gets filled with the Holy Spirit. As the word "Hallelujah!" springs from Rev. Mitchel's lips, Julia Ann leaps to her feet!

And as her legs extend, so do her arms—right into the sides of Ms. Lillie's and the lady's store-bought Sunday go-to meeting hats. And as the hats go tumbling into the aisle, so does Ms. Lillie's wig. Soon, Julia Ann is joined in her holy dance by DeEtta and Sara. And the entire church goes into a save a soul frenzy.

Rev. Mitchel later says, "That was the best service that we have had in a long time."

After church, DeEtta, Sara, and Julia Ann walk home together.

"Thanks!" DeEtta says as they are walking down the road a few yards in front of their parents.

"Thanks for what?" Julia Ann asks.

"For being my best friends," DeEtta replies.

CHAPTER 4

The Cemetery

S **ummer** 1990—The next morning, Mama Dee is awakened by the sound of people talking.

Stefan and the children must be here, she thinks as she sits up in the bed. She then slips into her house shoes and puts on her housecoat and heads for the elevator. After taking the elevator to the first floor, she heads to the kitchen where the voices are coming from.

As she walks into the room, she is greeted with kisses and hugs from her grandchildren. "Where is Stefan?" Mama Dee asks.

"He had to run to town to get something. He should be back in an hour or so," Clarice answers.

Mama Dee then turns her attention back to the children.

"Dad is going to get me a golf cart so that we can ride all over the place," Jamil, who has just turned thirteen, says. "It's going to be for my birthday," he adds.

"No, it's not! He said that it's going to be for all of us to ride. And that he is going to get it after your birthday. Not for your birthday!" Jamil's older sister Jazmin, who is fifteen, replies. Jazmin then asks Mama Dee, "Can I be the first one to give you a ride on it?" She then looks over at her brother and smiles to rub in the fact that she beat him to the punch.

As Jazmin and Jamil bicker back and forth about who's going to be the first to drive the golf cart, Clarice notices a man out back. He is off in the distance sitting on a lawnmower, cutting a section of grass.

"I wonder what he's out there cutting our grass for?" Clarice asks as she picks up her car keys and heads to her car. Jazmin and Jamil quickly hop in the car with her.

They are all in her car and gone before Mama Dee can get up and look out of the window to see what is happening. After looking out of the window, Mama Dee knows exactly what patch of grass he is cutting. It is the Shegogg family cemetery.

As she watches, Clarice drives the car up next to the man on the mower and lets down the car window. Clarice then says something to the man. And the man then says something back to Clarice.

Before long, Mama Dee can see from the house that Clarice and the man's conversation has become heated. After several exchanges, the man drives the lawnmower onto a small trailer hooked to a pickup truck, gets in, and drives off.

As Clarice is driving back toward the house, Mama Dee walks over to the chair that she was sitting in and sits back down. The sight of the Shegogg family cemetery jogs her memory once more and brings another piece of her past to the forefront of her thoughts.

* * *

1933—"Come on, get up out of that bed, sleepyhead! I know that you aren't asleep. I heard you sneaking around the house an hour ago," Mary says to DeEtta.

"Yeah! Me too!" Sandy Earl adds.

"Y'all, leave that girl alone. If she wants to sleep all day on her thirteenth birthday, she can go right ahead. I'll just take this gift we bought for her back to the store," Sonny says as he turns and pretends to walk out of the bedroom.

DeEtta pulls the covers from over her head and sits up in the bed with a massive smile on her face. "Come on, Daddy! Please don't take it back," she cries out.

Sonny reaches just outside of the bedroom door and pulls up a brown paper bag and hands it to Mary as she sits down on the bed next to DeEtta.

DeEtta is so excited that she can hardly get the string off of the wrapped gift inside of it. After unwrapping the gift, she reaches inside the box and pulls out a beautiful blue dress trimmed in white lace. "I bought the material from the Chinaman store up town. And I ordered the lace from the Sears and Roebuck store in Chicago," Mary says.

DeEtta is speechless. And as the tears of joy are flowing from her eyes, she puts both of her arms around her mother and squeezes her as if she had given her all the riches of the world. While still standing across the room, Sonny and Sandy Earl watch while trying to do what men were expected to do back then—hold back their tears.

After eating the huge breakfast that Mary has prepared, they all get dressed for church. DeEtta can't wait to show her friend the new dress that she got for her birthday. So, on that Sunday morning, she is the first one dressed.

As they walk into the church, Mary and Sonny let DeEtta walk a few paces ahead of them so that she can show off her new outfit. And as DeEtta walks down the center aisle of the church, she looks to see if her friends Julia Ann and Sara are there. She then smiles as she sees them sitting in their usual spots behind Ms. Lillie and her friends.

DeEtta motions with her head to tell them to move up front so that everyone can see her new outfit. Julia Ann and Sara both giggle as they get up and make their way toward the front of the church. As the three of them take seat up front behind Julia Ann's parents, Julia Ann's mother shakes her finger at them as a warning to keep quiet during the services.

While Rev. Mitchel preaches from the book of Revelation, DeEtta, Julia Ann, and Sara sit as still and keep as quiet as they can. And as the service ends, they all ask their parents if they can walk home together right then instead of waiting around while their parents talk and fellowship with the other church members.

"Daddy, would it be okay if I walk home with Julia Ann and Sara so that we can change clothes and have some time to play before dark?" DeEtta asks Sonny. Sonny looks over at Mary. And from the look that he gives her, she knows that he wants her to answer the question.

Mary sighs before saying, "Okay, but you girls go straight home and stay on the road. No shortcuts!"

DeEtta quickly agrees to her mother's terms and thanks them both before running off to tell her friends the good news.

As the girls walk down the road toward home, DeEtta tells her friends about the wonderful morning that she had and how excited she was when she saw the beautiful dress that her mother had made for her. They then talk about boys and how many children they want to have after they get married.

Before long, they come upon a path that leads off the road and into the woods. Sara asks, "Do y'all want to see something?"

"See what?" DeEtta asks.

"Some really old tombstones," Sara says.

"Now, why would anyone want to look some old dead folks' tombstones?" Julia Ann asks. "Besides, I was told that there are some albino opossums that live in that cemetery. And y'all know what albino opossums are?" Julia adds while moving her head from side to side.

"I think y'all are afraid. Scary cats! Scary cats! The kind of cat that won't chase a rat!" Sara sings as DeEtta and Julia Ann contemplate doing what their parents had told them not to do.

"We're not afraid. We just don't want to see no dead people graves," DeEtta says.

"Or any albino opossums that's going to take our souls straight to hell," Julia quickly adds.

And just as they start to continue their journey home, John Jr., who is now seventeen years old and Steven, who is now sixteen come riding down the path on their horses. John Jr. is on a large white horse that he calls

General Lee. As General Lee runs past the girls, his thunderous hooves send dust and dirt high into the air and all over DeEtta's new dress as the horse reacts to John Jr. hitting it on its backside with the switch from a tree that he has in his hand.

After racing past the girls, John Jr. pulls back hard on the horse's reins, causing it to rear up as it comes to a stop. And as the horse's hooves touch the ground, John Jr. dismounts. "Where are you girls headed?" he asks.

The girls attempt to keep walking but are cut off by General Lee as John Jr. pulls him around in front of them and blocks their path.

"We're going home," Julia Ann says as she and her friends back away from John Jr. and the huge horse.

"Julia Ann, why don't you come on and take a walk with me?" John Jr. says as he releases the horse's reins and grabs her by the hand and pulls her toward the path that goes through the woods toward the cemetery, the smell of alcohol practically filling the air each time he exhales. DeEtta and Sara grab Julia Ann by the other arm and pulls as hard as they can in the opposite direction.

"Turn her loose!" John Jr. shouts as he continues to pull. But neither Sara nor DeEtta pay him any mind. They just keep on holding on to their friend's arm while crying for help.

After seeing what his brother was trying to do, Steven comes charging by on his horse Diamond. He sticks out his leg as he rides past and kicks his brother squarely in the side of his face, knocking him to the ground. And as John Jr. gets back to his feet, dazed and staggering, Steven makes another pass.

This time, he places his boot dead in the center of his brother's chest, knocking him back to the ground. Steven then jumps off of his horse and says to the girls, "Y'all go on home." And as DeEtta, Sara, and Julia run back down the trail toward the road, the brothers fight one another as if they are Cain and Abel.

While running, DeEtta looks up at the Shegogg's sprawling Southern mansion, which sits on top of the highest hill on the land. And while looking at the house, she sees Kathy May Shegogg sitting on the balcony looking out toward the cemetery. While continuing to run, DeEtta wonders, *What kind of mother would sit and watch her son do something like that and does nothing to stop it?*

After making it to DeEtta's house, Sara and Julia Ann help DeEtta clean the dirt from her new dress. While doing so, they promise one another that they will never tell a soul about what had happened on the trail near the Shegogg family cemetery that day because they all know if their parents ever find out what had happened, they will never be able to go anywhere alone for a long, long time.

CHAPTER 5

The Harvest Festival

Summer 1990—"Come and take a ride with me, Mama Dee, I have something to show you," Jamil says as he pulls up on the golf cart that had just been delivered earlier that morning.

"What in the world do you have to show me?" Mama Dee asks as she steps down off of the porch.

"It's a really old car! I found it in the old barn on the other side of the field. It looks like it was in pretty good shape. That is, until part of the roof of the barn collapsed on it. You want to see it?" Jamil asks.

"No, not today. Maybe we'll do it some other time," Mama Dee says as she is walking over to a bench setting under the large oak tree that stands tall in the front yard.

After sitting down on the bench, she pulls out her paper fan and starts to fan herself. Jamil circles the tree with the golf cart as he continues to try and convince her to take that ride with him.

"Boy! I am not going to ride on that thing today. And to be perfectly honest with you, I might not ride on it tomorrow or the next day either. But I will tell you what you can do for me. Why don't you ride that thing around back and go into the kitchen and bring me a nice cold Coca-Cola? Now that's something you can do for your Mama Dee!" she says.

Jamil laughs as he heads off to retrieve her Coca-Cola.

After a while, Jazmin comes out of the house and sits down beside her. "What are you doing, Mama Dee?" Jazmin asks.

"Just sitting here waiting on your brother to bring me a Coca-Cola," she answers.

Just then, Jamil comes flying around the corner of the house on the cart. He pulls up next to the bench and reaches out to hand her the soda.

"Can you open it for me?" Mama Dee asks.

"Sure!" Jamil replies. As he pulls the tab on the can, he gets immediately drenched by a soda pop geyser as the soda sprays right into his face.

Mama Dee then says, "And that is why you never shake up a Coca-Cola. Now go and get me another one. And this time, slow that darn thing down!"

Meanwhile, Jazmin is practically rolling on the ground, laughing. "See! That's what you get for hogging the golf cart," she says while continuing to chuckle. As Jamil heads back to the kitchen to retrieve another soda, Mama Dee smiles—just a little.

"Mama Dee, I remember you saying that you and Poppa had been together for almost forever. But you never told me about how you two got together," Jazmin says.

Mama Dee's face ignites up with a smile so big that Jazmin can tell that just the thought of her and Marcus being together brings her heart a joy that travels throughout her soul. "I was just fifteen years old when we knew that we were meant to be together," Mama Dee says as she starts to blush.

* * *

Late Fall 1935—"Please, Mama, everybody is going to be there. And I promise not to leave Sandy Earl's sight. And besides, Julia Ann and Sara's mamas are letting them go," DeEtta says as she tries to convince Mary to let her go to the Harvest Fest, which happens every year at the end of the picking season.

"Well, let me talk to your dad and see what he says," Mary replies. DeEtta knows that if she can only get her mother to agree with her going, it is practically a done deal because her father's go-to reply to most things that her mother asks him about pertaining to her and her brother is "What do you think, Mary?"

So that night when Sony and Sandy Earl get home from the fields, DeEtta helps her mother set the table for dinner. The food is hot and on the table waiting for them.

After seeing that the food already on the table, Sonny starts to wonder if he had forgotten an anniversary or maybe a birthday. After giving Mary a kiss, he awkwardly looks at her in the hope that she will give him some kind of clue of what the occasion was before declaring that he has forgotten it or that it wasn't important enough for him to have remembered.

Still hoping for a clue from Mary, Sonny sits down. And just as they are starting to eat, he asks, "So what is the special occasion?"

"Oh, there is no special occasion. DeEtta unexpectedly helped out in the kitchen and that made things move a little faster than anticipated.

"Um…" Sonny replies as a feeling of relief falls over him.

After dinner, Sonny steps out onto the front porch and takes a seat in his favorite rocking chair and lights up his pipe. While helping her mother wash the dishes, DeEtta slowly and meticulously wipes one of the plates that her mother has just finished washing with a dry cloth. As she is drying the plate, she looks up at her with a sad set of puppy dog eyes.

Knowing what she wants, Mary looks over at her and then back down at what she is doing and starts to hum one of her favorite church songs. After finishing the dishes, DeEtta's face lights up when Mary goes out and sits with Sonny on the front porch.

"How is the picking coming along?" Mary asks as she sits down in the other rocking chair next to Sonny.

"It's coming along," Sonny says as he takes a puff from his pipe." Mary starts to hum one of her church songs once more.

"What's the matter?" Sonny asks.

"Nothing. Just sitting here thinking about how fast our kids are growing up. You know, DeEtta will be sixteen years old this year. Today she asked me if she could go to the harvest party with her brother. I was going to tell her no right off the bat, but then I started to think about back when we were young," Mary says as she places her hand on the arm of Sonny's rocking chair on top of his hand.

Sonny looks over at his wife and smiles as he, too, starts to recall their younger days. He then asks her, "What do you think about her going?"

"I think we have done a good job of raising her. And it's time for us to let her start experiencing some of what life has to offer," Mary answers.

The Harvest Fest was a day-long picnic and party put on at the end of the cotton picking season. The big land-owners would rotate, supplying the hog for the roasting and the shed or barn for the dance that followed. This particular year, the festival is being held at Mr. Yancy's place, which happens to be the second largest farm in the area, second to only the Shegogg's place, which is, by far, the largest. The two farms are about five miles apart and share many of the same business practices, especially when it comes to the sharecroppers.

After the picnic, some people would go home to change clothes in preparation for the party that followed. And usually, a lot of the older people didn't come back to the party because some felt that all that dancing and drinking was better suited for the young. And then there were the others, like Ms. Lillie. They felt that it wasn't Christian like to drink and strut your stuff like that, so they would stay home as well. But the young and the young at heart had a saying that went, "The picnic is for the old, and the party is for the new. Come sundown, put on your fanciest duds, and let us see what you can do."

On the day of the Harvest Fest, DeEtta, Sara, and Julia all dress as close alike as they can. They want everyone to be able to tell that they're together and that they are best friends.

As they are waiting to leave, Mary says, "You girls sure look nice in your pretty white and blue dresses." She and Sonny are standing on the front porch of their house looking at them while they wait on Sandy Earl to finish hitching up the mules and bring the wagon down from the stable.

After everyone is loaded into the wagon, Sandy Earl signals to the mules to get moving. Mary and the other two girls' mothers wave to their daughters as they all head off to their first adult party without them. As the mule-drawn wagon makes its way down the pothole-infested road, off in the far distance, the sun can be seen slowly but continuously making its departure from the autumn sky.

"Do you all have any room on that wagon for us?" Marcus asks as Sandy Earl and the girls ride past his house. Marcus is accompanied by Jimmy and Jimmy's female cousin Brenda, who is down visiting from St Louis, Missouri.

"Sure! Hop on in," Sandy Earl says as he brings the wagon to a stop.

Marcus helps Brenda onto the front seat of the wagon next to Sandy Earl. He then hops in the back of the wagon and sits between DeEtta and Julia. Jimmy sits across from them next to Sara. And as they ride off into the setting sun, the mood becomes that of the early pages of a romance novel in which each one of them has their own starring role to play.

As the wagon pulls up to the barn where the party is, they see Steven Shegogg standing off at a distance, watching. Most of the partygoers pay no significant attention to him because they all know that Steven is the complete opposite of his brother. Ever since he and his brother John Jr. had the fight by the cemetery, he would come around from time to time and just watch them from afar. It is as if he wants to say something or be a part of what is going on at the time but just doesn't know how to say it or even know what it was that he needs to say.

After everyone gets off of the wagon, Sandy Earl takes it around to the back of the barn and ties off the mules.

While DeEtta, Sara, Brenda, and Julia all stand out front strategizing on how they are going to make their entrance into the party, Steven Shegogg makes his way over to them. "How are you nice ladies doing tonight?" he asks.

All of them are stunned speechless except for Julia, who is the eldest of the three. She replies, "We are doing just fine. And how are you doing, Mr. Shegogg?"

Steven, who has just recently turned eighteen, looks down toward the ground because he is somewhat hurt that she feels she needs to call him mister. After some hesitation, he replies, "Please don't ever call me that. My name is Steven."

"We are doing fine…Steven. And how are you doing?" Julia replies as they both smile while looking at each other.

DeEtta pulls Julia's arm, signaling to her that it is time to go inside to the party and stop smiling in that white boy's face. Julia wipes the smile from her face as she looks over at DeEtta, who has a "You got to be kidding me!" look on her face." Sara doesn't say a word. She is still processing the part about when Steven said he didn't want them calling him mister any more.

Julia looks back over at Steven and smiles once more as she says, "Goodbye!"

The girls then head into the party, leaving Steven Shegogg just standing there looking at Julia as she walks away.

"I can't believe you looked at him like that," DeEtta says to Julia. "In case you forgot—*and* lost your eyesight, he is a Shegogg—*and* he is white," DeEtta says as she continues to scold her friend for her behavior.

"Would you ladies like to dance?" Marcus asks as he, Sandy Earl, and Jimmy walk over and stand next to them.

"Sure!" Julia says as she quickly takes Sandy Earl by the hand and pulls him out on the dance floor so that she can get away from DeEtta and her chastising.

After the partygoers dance late into the night, the mood of the party changes from one that was charged with the electricity of foot-stamping, fast-paced music to a more somber atmosphere of slow music and whispers of romance.

"You sure do look beautiful in that dress that you are wearing tonight," Marcus says to DeEtta, taking her by the hand as they are walking past the stable where the wagon is parked.

"Why, thank you, Marcus. It's very nice of you to notice," DeEtta replies as they stop walking and turn to face one another.

"Those stars up there sure are pretty tonight. And I think they might be twinkling just for us," Marcus says as he makes his move and tries to kiss DeEtta.

DeEtta pushes away and replies, "I don't think that those stars are twinkling for me. They twinkle just to be twinkling. No matter if something good or bad is about to happen, they just twinkle. I really don't look at them much anymore." DeEtta then turns and starts walking back toward the party.

Marcus takes DeEtta by the hand and turns her so that they are facing each other once more and says, "DeEtta, I have had my eyes on you ever since we were little kids. And I have truly come to admire everything about you. The way you wear your hair, the way you talk, even the way you walk down the road. Seeing it all just makes me feel a special kind of way whenever you come around. And most of the time, when I'm alone, out in the fields chopping cotton, or bailing hay, it is the thoughts of you that fill my lonesomeness."

Marcus and DeEtta then kiss as a large horned owl that is roosting in the tree above where they are standing starts to hoot at the autumn moon that is glowing in the night sky.

After kissing, Marcus asks, "DeEtta, will you be my girl, forever and forever and forever?"

DeEtta smiles as a single tear of joy rolls down her cheek. And she replies, "And forever and forever."

CHAPTER 6

Up Town

Summer 1990—Later on the same day, Clarice asks the question, "Who all wants to go out for dinner?"

And although it is about a twenty-five-mile drive to get to a nice restaurant, Jazmin and Jamil quickly answer, "Yes! We do." They start heading toward the car before Mama Dee can register a vote or even say a word.

After Jazmin and Jamil resolve the question of who will get to ride in the front seat, they all get into the car and head toward the restaurant. While driving along, Jazmin and Jamil start to talk about how things must have been around these parts back when Mama Dee was young.

And as the two of them sat in the back seat discussing what Mama Dee's past must have been like, Clarice asks, "Who wants to see the town that Grandma grew up in?"

Both children quickly answer, "We do!" as they exit through the gate at the entrance to their property.

Mama Dee sits quietly in the front seat and thinks to herself, *I probably could count the number of times I went to town while living here as a child. It was something that we had little desire to do back then. And when I was a child, our parents had downright forbidden it,* she recalls. But for the sake of the conversation, she doesn't even try and correct Clarice's statement.

After a short drive, they come to a flashing yellow light that is located at the corner of Main Street and Jefferson Davis Ave, which is where the town's city limits begin. As they drive through the center of the small town, Mama Dee recognizes a lot of the old structures that are still standing that were there when she was young.

Most of them are abandoned and badly run down, but they are still standing and recognizable. The most recognizable places are the old drug store, the building that was once the sheriff's office, and the empty lot where the cloth and sewing material store once stood. The cloth and sewing material store were owned by the only Chinese family that lived in the area at the time. It was referred to by pretty much everybody back then as "the Chinamen store."

But the structure that sticks out the most is the one that had been there long before the others. It is the building that housed the Shegogg family's store and bank. This building was once the epicenter for the sharecropper's day-to-day perishable and financial needs and the only source for the items that couldn't be grown in their fields and gardens.

The reason that this building stands out most to Mama Dee is not because of the way it looks or its size. It is because it had been the monumental reason for a lot of the sharecroppers' inability to prosper from their often backbreaking labor by using unregulated floating interest rates, manipulating or downright inflating the amounts of the sharecroppers' debts, combined with forcing the sharecroppers who lived on their property to only shop in their stores and only come to them for loans or face being evicted from their land. It literally became the tool that kept a lot of the sharecroppers not only in line but forever in their debt. And this created a constant state of indebted servitude for many of them.

The forcing of all the sharecroppers who lived on the old plantation to shop at the same store and use the same bank forced a lot of them to intermingle and become somewhat dependent on one another. And to keep from having to borrow money from the landowner, they would borrow from each other and pool their cash together when shopping. And instead of buying five pounds of sugar for thirty cents, they would buy a fifty-pound sack for two dollars and divide it up among themselves.

They would almost always go to town in groups. This was not only an economical way to get the thing that they needed, but it was also the safest way of doing it because being caught alone on a lonely dark road at night by a group of drunk white men was not the place that any person of color wanted to find themselves back then.

In Mama Dee's eyes, the town looks the same in some aspects and different in others. The skyline is the same, but the people walking the streets have changed. The middle-aged and young white people who once went about their daily business have been replaced by people of color, most of them teenagers and senior citizens. Many of the young blacks are males, and they stand around as if they have nowhere in particular to be or are just waiting for something to happen.

This is a huge contrast to what had been the norm back when Mama Dee was young. It is as if someone or something had removed a portion of the intimidation that Jim Crow had allowed, and taken all of the opportunities and resources for economic advancement with it.

"What do you think, Mama Dee?" Clarice asks as she tries to get her to add something to the ongoing back and forth conversation that Jazmin and Jamil are having.

"I'm sorry, I really haven't been paying attention. I've just been sitting here taking in the scenery," she replies while continuing to look out of the window as she recalls what had happened to them on one of their family trips town back when she was a young girl.

* * *

Winter 1935—"I can't remember the last time we got this much snow down here," Nathan says as he hitches one of the mules up to the wagon.

"Who's all riding to town with us this morning?" Sonny asks as he brings the other mule from the barn.

"Ms. Lillie wanted to ride with us, but I asked Sara to go by and get some money and a list of what she needed. Sara can shop for her things while we get the other stuff," Nathan replies.

"Would it be okay if Mary and DeEtta ride along? Mary wants to pick up a few things from the Chinamen store," Sonny says.

"Sure! The only other person that going is Jimmy," Nathan replies.

The howling sound made by wind makes the chill in the air feel all the more menacing. And the tiny bits of falling snow seem to be searching for any speck of uncovered flush to land on to remind you of just how cold it really is. The wagon full of sharecroppers makes its way down the trail toward town as the wind blows across the wide open snow-covered fields.

After making it to town, Nathan drops Mary and DeEtta off at the cloth store and then heads over to the Shegogg's store to shop for the other things that they need. No sooner does Mr. Loo see Mary walk in through the door that he and his wife drop what they are doing and run over to her.

Mary and the Loos had become good friends over the years, and they are always happy to see her. Mary has done a little sewing for them from time to time.

"How is our favorite customer doing today?" Mrs. Loo asks in broken but understandable English as she reaches out for Mary's hand.

"We are doing fine. And yourselves?" Mary asks.

"Wonderfully!" Mrs. Loo replies.

After looking at what the Loos have to offer as far as selection, Mary puts in an order for a pattern she found in one of their numerous catalogs. She and DeEtta then head over to the Shegogg's store. As they are walking past some of the other stores. DeEtta and her mother do a little window shopping.

While standing in front of the five-and-dime store looking at a set of kitchen pots and pans that are being displayed in the window, DeEtta sees John Jr. and three of his friends coming down the road in their direction.

Mary glances at them but doesn't really pay them much attention. But on the other hand, DeEtta knows that whenever you see John Jr., there is potential for trouble.

"How y'all ladies doing this morning?" John Jr. asks as he and his friends walk up.

"Just fine," Mary replies before looking up and noticing that it is John Jr. she is talking to. The other boys snicker as if they had some discussion about what they were going to do or say to them once they walked up on them.

John Jr. then asks a question. It is a question that he damn well knows the answer to before asking it.

"Don't y'all live on our place?" he asks while starring at DeEtta.

And as the other boys giggle like a pack of hyenas toying with their prey before eating it, Mary replies, "Yes, sir, we do." She then takes DeEtta by the hand and pulls her around behind her.

"Come, come, you forgot something!" Mr. Loo shouts out while he is standing at the front door of his store. He then waves his hand in the air, signaling for Mary and DeEtta to come back to the store.

"Excuse us," Mary says as she and DeEtta step out into the road and walk through the slushy mud to go around John Jr. and his friends.

As they walk back into the store, Mr. Loo says, "That John Jr. nothing but trouble. You and DeEtta stay in here until your husband come and get you."

Mrs. Loo goes into the back of the store and brings back a pot of hot tea. And as DeEtta and Mary wait for

Nathan and Sonny to come back with the wagon to pick them up, they sit and talk with Mrs. Loo.

During the ride home, DeEtta thinks for sure that her mother would tell her father about what had happened on the street that morning. But Mary doesn't say a word about it. Mary knows that it would force her husband, whom she loves as much as she loves life itself, to do something that would probably get him killed. And that would leave her alone with their two children to make it in a world that seemed hell-bent on destroying them and everybody who looked like them.

As the wagon makes its way toward home, DeEtta watches as her mother takes her father by the hand and lays her head on his shoulder. And on that late evening, during a snowstorm in the winter of 1935, DeEtta comes to a similar conclusion.

And while riding in the back of a crowded wagon on the way home from town that cold winter day, DeEtta talks about a lot of things. She talks about the weather, the pattern that she and her mother had picked out while in the Chinamen store. She even talks a little bit about the coming planting season.

Although, the events that took place down the street from the Chinamen store will be forever etched in DeEtta's memory. On that frigid day, while riding in the wagon, they never come across her lips.

CHAPTER 7

A Truth

Summer 1990—"Are you going to lay in that bed all day?" Mama Dee asks as she pulls back the curtain covering the window, allowing the rays from the sun to come beaming into Jazmin's bedroom. Jazmin pulls the sheet back up over her head, but Mama Dee pulls it right back off again.

"Get out of that bed and go downstairs and eat some breakfast! You'll feel so much better," Mama Dee says as she starts to pull the linen from the bed to throw it into a pile of dirty clothes on the floor that she is about to wash.

"Shouldn't the housekeeper be doing that?" Jazmin asks as she sits up on the side of the bed.

"See! That's why you kids are so lazy! Your parents never make you do anything. Now get up off of that bed and go downstairs so that I can finish stripping it!" Mama Dee says as she picks up the pile of dirty linen and heads toward the next bedroom.

Jazmin can hear the scenario being repeated as Mama Dee enters Jamil's room. After sitting on the side of the bed for a few more minutes, Jazmin gets up and goes into her bathroom and washes her face and brushes her teeth before heading downstairs to the kitchen. As she walks down the stairs, her nose is greeted with the delightful aroma of bacon, eggs, and cooked apples. She has not had the pleasure of being greeted by smells like that since the last time that she and her brother spent the night at Mama Dee's house back when they all were still living in Detroit.

As she steps into the kitchen, she sees that her brother has beat her there. And not only has he already fixed himself a plate, but he is well into the process of devouring every morsel.

"Did you even wash your hands? I know that you didn't brush your teeth because I didn't hear any water running in your bathroom," Jazmin says to her brother as she gets a plate from the cabinet.

"What are you? The hall monitor or something?" Jamil replies as he continues to eat.

"No, I'm not the hall monitor, but I am going to tell Mama Dee when she comes down stairs. Now, what do you have to say to that, smarty pants?" Jazmin says while fixing her plate.

"Snitches, stitches, and bitches. They all go together!" Jamil says as he gets up from the table and brushes against her as he walks out of the kitchen.

"Now I have two things to tell her when she comes down! And we will see who's going to need stitches," Jazmin replies as she starts to eat.

"What are you kids fighting about now?" Mama Dee asks as she walks into the kitchen.

"That wasn't me, Mama Dee, it was Jamil. And he was using foul language," Jazmin explains.

"I was not doing any such a thing," Jamil says just before Mama Dee pops him upside his head.

"That was for using the foul language and trying to lie about it. I heard you from the other room," Mama Dee says. "Now Jazmin, you finish eating, and Jamil, you go get your shower and get back down here before your parents get home. Their plane landed in Memphis about twenty minutes ago. So they will be here in about an hour," Mama Dee says as she starts to clean up the kitchen. Jazmin and Jamil continue to argue as Jamil heads toward the stairs.

Sometime later, Clarice and Stefan walk through the door.

"How was your trip?" Mama Dee asks.

"It was great! He worked while I shopped," Clarice says while displaying a huge smile. Stefan doesn't say anything. He just grabs the suitcases and take them upstairs.

Clarice starts to say something to him, but after seeing the look on his face, she quickly decides not to. "He needs a little more time to finish processing it all," Clarice says to Mama Dee. Mama Dee doesn't say a word; she just goes back into the kitchen and sits down by the window. Clarice follows her into the kitchen and sits down beside her.

"You know what the sad thing is?" Mama Dee asks.

"What's that?" Clarice replies. "For the last forty-five years, I have replayed what happened over and over again in my head. And I just can't seem to find or even see which part I could have changed that would have made things come out right," Mama Dee says.

"Mama Dee, there is one thing that I know for sure. And that is, Stefan loves you more than any child could ever love their mother. So please, for his sake. Let's give it some more time," Clarice says. She then gets up, hugs Mama Dee, and kisses her on the cheek before heading upstairs to talk with Stefan.

* * *

Early Fall 1937—The rain starts suddenly and quickly turns into a blinding downpour. As DeEtta and Marcus race toward his house, he holds his jacket out over her head in a futile attempt to keep her dry. As they both finally make it onto his porch, they are both wringing wet. Marcus quickly goes inside and starts a fire.

As they both stand dripping wet looking at the fireplace, DeEtta asks, "Do you have anything dry that I can put on while my clothes dry?"

Marcus stutters as he replies, "I'm sure that there is something around here that you could borrow." He then goes into the other room of the tiny shack and looks through a trunk containing his mother's things.

After a short while, he emerges from the room with an old housecoat that has been patched in several places. He hands it to DeEtta and tells her that she can go into the room and change.

While changing out of her wet clothes, DeEtta asks, "Where are your parents?"

Marcus quickly replies, "They went to town with Jimmy and his father. They won't be heading back this way until after it stops raining, so you don't need to rush."

After undressing down to her underwear, DeEtta asks Marcus to pass her the towel that is lying on the back of the chair in the front room. Marcus, who has also started to remove his wet clothes, picks up the towel and takes it over to her. DeEtta partly opens the door and sticks her arm through the opening while keeping her almost naked body hidden behind the door.

She then slowly sticks her head around and peeks through the opening. She is stirred when she sees Marcus's wet, shirtless body, noticing how the long, labor-intensive days of working in the fields have shaped and sculptured it into something that is not only physically arousing to look at but alluring to the touch as well. His muscular chest and arms glisten in the dimly lit room as the crackling flames in the fireplace dance and cast manipulated shadows onto the various surfaces of his dripping, wet body.

DeEtta's heart starts to pulsate as thoughts of making love for the first time push their way into her mind. After continuing to gaze at Marcus's wet and masculine body, her desires take control. And her heart and her actions become one as she pushes the door open.

Marcus just stands there motionless as he takes in the beauty of each and every smooth and voluptuous inch of her body. And in one fluid motion, he gently takes her into his strong arms, lifting her from the floor. He lays her softly on the homemade mattress lying in the corner of the front room where he sleeps. And as the sound of the falling rain drowns out the distant sounds of thunder as the storm settles in, Marcus and DeEtta consummate their love for one another.

After the rain ends, DeEtta and Marcus get dressed, and he walks her home. While holding hands and walking through the misty fog that has rolled in as the rains retreat to the distant countryside, they talk about things like what a future together would be like and the number of children that they wanted.

Once they reach the top of a hill, they can see the tops of the row of houses that DeEtta and her family live in pierce up through the fog.

"I think that I had better walk alone from here because if Poppa sees that we are together, we might be in trouble. Because I've been gone all day," DeEtta says.

"So…what are you going to tell him if he asks you where you've been all day?" Marcus asks.

"If he asks, I'll tell him I was with Julia at her house when the rain started, and we just hung out until it stopped," DeEtta says as she kisses Marcus and sends him on his way.

As DeEtta continues to walk, she hears laughter and conversation off in the distance. But the fog is so thick that she can hardly see more than twenty or thirty feet in front of her. She then hears the sound of a horse riding off in the other direction. And as she reaches the first house in the row of houses, she sees her friend Julia coming down the road toward her.

"And where in the world are you coming from?" Julia asks.

"From Marcus's house, but if anybody asks, I was with you," DeEtta says. "And where are you coming from? And who were you talking to?" DeEtta asks.

"I'm coming from Sara's house. And I wasn't talking to anyone," Julia replies.

"I could have sworn that I heard voices coming from the direction you just came from," DeEtta says.

"Girl, I think you just hearing things. And walking alone in this creepy old fog doesn't help," Julia replies.

"I agree. You want to stay at my house until it clears?" DeEtta asks.

"Sure!" Julia answers. They both then head off to DeEtta's house.

CHAPTER 8
Marcus's Car

S ummer 1990—"Mama Dee? Who is that in the picture with you?" Jazmin asks while looking around on Mama Dee's Dresser.

"Those are my friends Sara and Julia Ann. Well…It was my friend Julia Ann. She is now deceased. Actually, she was my best friend," Mama Dee replies after a brief hesitation.

"That sure looks like a really old picture. Was that your car that you all are standing next to?" Jazmin asks.

"Actually! That was your grandfather's first car. We weren't married at the time," Mama Dee answers. "If I remember right, I believe he worked on that car more than we rode in it," Mama Dee adds with a smile as she recalls the day when the picture was taken. She then goes on to tell Jazmin the story about the car.

* * *

Summer 1938—While many of the sharecroppers living in the row of houses along the road sit on their front porches trying to escape the dreaded summer heat. They are all treated to a most hilarious sight on this hot July evening. Marcus and Jimmy Lee come rolling down the road atop a wagon drawn by a pair of mules.

The sight of them on a wagon pulled by a pair of mules is not all that unusual. What's strange is what is attached to the wagon and the stir that it's creating. Marcus has bought himself a 1928 Ford...or at least a good portion of one.

The driver's door to the car is lying in the back seat, all four tires are flat, and the headlights are dangling by the wires. And these are only the things that one can see. As the mule-drawn spectacle makes its way down the road, it gives the tiny community a break from the boredom of just sitting around in the heat waiting for a cool breeze to blow.

As the precession passes, everyone waves to DeEtta, who is sitting behind the steering wheel, steering the contraption as they make their way down the wagon wheel rut-infested road. After passing the first couple of houses, they are joined in the rear by a group of children with sticks banging on old lard and molasses buckets. And by the time they make it past the last of the houses, it looks as if a ragtag parade has come to pay the small enclave of sharecroppers a visit.

Most of the Black residents of the Shegogg place had never been inside of an actual automobile before let alone know someone firsthand who actually owned one. Therefore, running or not, it is a first for the entire community. Marcus stops the wagon in front of his parents' house and unhooks the car from the wagon. And as he and Jimmy start to push the car back alongside the house, Steven Shegogg rides up on his horse.

Steven had been watching all of the excitement from afar and wants to get a closer look at the automobile. "Nice car," Steven says, smiling as he climbs down off of his horse.

"I know it needs a little TLC, but thanks anyway for the kind word," Marcus replies as he and Jimmy finish pushing the car.

Over the past couple of years, Steven and most of the sharecroppers have developed a somewhat mutual relationship of respect. And he and Marcus have become what some folks might even call friends.

"I know where there is another old Ford at that you might be able to get some parts off of," Steven says as he, Jimmy, and Marcus look under the hood.

Before long, a group of the sharecroppers that live in the houses that are scattered on the hillside come walking down the road to see Marcus's car. Julia, who could hardly wait to talk to DeEtta and kid her about driving a car being drawn by a wagon and mules, quickly joins the precession as it passes. As the crowd gathers around the car, Julia stands next to DeEtta and Marcus.

"Hi, how you doing, Julia Ann?" Steven says in a voice loud enough for only Marcus, DeEtta, and Julia to hear.

"Just fine, Steven," Julia replies while continuing to look at the car. DeEtta acts as if she is not paying attention as she continues to talk to Marcus.

For the next two weeks, Marcus works on that car every day after coming home from the fields. Steven and Jimmy come over and help when they can. But with their help or not, Marcus is determined to get it running. Then one day, like a phoenix rising from the ashes, it is finally time to turn the key and see if she'll start. Marcus asks DeEtta to do the honors. And after a lot of pumping the gas pedal and priming the carburetor, it starts. Marcus tells DeEtta to scoot over, and he quickly jumps behind the wheel. And as the car goes zigzagging down the road, Marcus and DeEtta grin from ear to ear.

The following day is a Sunday, so Marcus offers DeEtta and her parents a ride to church. DeEtta tells Marcus that her parents had kindly and respectfully turned him down. So he asks Jimmy, Sara, and Julia to ride with them instead.

While riding to church, Marcus asks DeEtta, "Why didn't your parents want to ride with us? Are they afraid of cars?"

DeEtta replies, "No, it's not the car that they are afraid of. When I asked Papa, he said a few swear words and then mumbled something about, 'The way that damn fool drive. I'll be damned if your mother and I are going to be in that contraption when he runs it into a tree and kills himself and whoever else that is crazy enough to be riding with him at the time.'"

As the car pulls up to the church. Over half the congregation is standing out front waiting to see Marcus's car. Marcus quickly hops out and runs around to the other side and opens DeEtta's door. After DeEtta and the others get out of the car, they all walk into the church together. Marcus tries to act as if it's no big deal, but DeEtta has a smile on her face that is so big one would think that they had just stepped out of a brand-new Duesenberg.

During church service, Rev. Mitchel is even able to find a parable in the Bible that he can relate to Marcus getting a car. After church, Marcus, DeEtta, Jimmy, Sara, and Julia go for a ride. And as they are cruising down the road, Marcus honks his horn as he passes a wagon loaded with hay being pulled by a team of mules. The wagon driver waves and smiles at them as they zoom past.

Not long after leaving the church, they find themselves in the middle of town and among plenty of better-looking cars. But only a few are actually owned by persons of color. Marcus pulls his car over and parks in front of the Chinamen store. Mrs. Loo sees DeEtta sitting in the front passenger seat and runs out to greet her. Although Mr. and Mrs. Loo owns a brand-new car that they very seldom drive, they both say to Marcus, "What a nice car you have there."

Even though the paint job is lacking, along with several other very noticeable issues like missing rear door handles, cracked windshield, etc., the Loos knew how much of a big deal it must be to Marcus to even have a car. So, as far as the other issues, they just looked past them and pretended that they didn't even notice.

After talking to the Loos, Marcus, DeEtta, and Julia start to get back into the car.

"Hold on a minute!" Mrs. Loo asks. She then runs back into the store and comes back out with a camera. "I want to take a picture of you three lovely ladies with your beautiful dresses on," she says. DeEtta, Sara, and Julia pose next to Marcus's car while Mrs. Loo takes the picture. After developing the image, Mrs. Loo gives the photo to DeEtta and says, "Good times should always be remembered."

They all then get into the car and head for home. While driving down the road with the wind blowing in her face, DeEtta thinks about what Mrs. Loo said and knows that each and every time she looks at that picture, she will be reminded of what a good time looks and feels like.

CHAPTER 9

Nothing Left to Give

Summer 1990—After eating dinner, Mama Dee and Jazmin go for a walk.

While walking down the driveway, Jazmin asks Mama Dee, "How well did you know the people who lived in this house back when you were young?"

Mama Dee replies, "I really couldn't say that I knew them very well at all, per se."

"But I thought you said that you grew up on this property," Jazmin says.

"I did, and so did a lot of other Black people. But the people who lived in this house happened to have been White. They owned all of this land, the houses along the road and on the hillside, and most of the livestock. We just rented from them and sharecropped with them. The sharecroppers typically kept to themselves most of the time," Mama Dee explains.

"What is sharecropping?" Jazmin asks as she takes Mama Dee by the hand.

After giving it a bit of thought, Mama Dee replies, "For us back then, it was a lot of hard work and very little pay or appreciation. If you got paid! Because sometimes there were people who didn't get paid what they were owed. In many cases, the people who paid you would try to tell you what to do with the little money that you earned."

"You are kidding. Could they do that, Mama Dee?" Jazmin asks with a surprised look on her face.

Mama Dee stops and looks at Jazmin. And as Jazmin stops and looks back at her, she says, "My dear sweet granddaughter. Back then, there was something called Jim Crow! Now, this Jim Crow wasn't a man or a thing. But it could be felt each and every time it wanted to reach out and touch you. It wasn't a place or a feeling, yet it was everywhere! All of the time! It was embedded in courts, the police, the stores, and even within us in the form of fear.

"This Jim Crow gave white people a lot of power over us and people who look like us for a lot of years. After some laws were passed, some of us got past our fear of it, even though a lot of the people who had enjoyed and prospered from that power continued to convince themselves that we were somehow inferior humans and that the only thing that we are good for is to serve and obey them. Even after we had been supposedly 'freed.'

"My parents, your great grandparents, and their parents and grandparents lived on this land. And no! They didn't really know the people who lived in this house either, although the people who lived in this house had as many generations live there as you did on this land. Getting to know us wasn't what they wanted to do. At least not the kind of knowing that you are talking about."

As they walk back to the house, there isn't much conversation. Jazmin processes the things that Mama Dee told her.

* * *

Fall of 1938—"Y'all boys can go ahead and get out of here, Nathan and I will finish up with the cotton weigh-in," Sonny says as he looks over at Sandy Earl and Jimmy, who can't wait to get done so that they can go and catch up with their friends.

Nathan smiles and shakes his head while helping Sonny pull the last sack of cotton from the wagon. Sandy Earl and Jimmy both thank their fathers as they take off toward the house.

"Those boys don't have nothing but pussy on their minds," Nathan says.

"You mean kind of like we did when we were their age," Sonny says as the both of them start laughing.

After getting the cotton weighed, Sonny and Nathan head inside to settle up with Big John. Nathan walks up to the counter first and gives Big John his slip of paper. Big John looks at the slip of paper, writes something in his book and on the slip of paper, and gives it back to Nathan. After Nathan is done, Sonny gives his slip of paper to Big John.

After looking at the slip of paper, Big John looks at his book and sees that Sonny's store account and rent is all paid up for the year and that he has over $400.00 owed to him. After seeing that, Big John asks, "Would you like

62

for me to hold on to what you got coming and use it on your rent as it comes due?"

"No, sir, Mr. Shegogg. I'd like to do like I done in the past, if you don't mind, sir," Sonny replies.

"Okay!" says Big John as he closes the book to prevent Sonny from seeing what is written in it.

After getting his money, Sonny and Nathan pick up their empty cotton sacks and walk outside and put them in the wagon. Sonny asks Nathan, "Are you in a hurry? If not, I'm going to walk across the street and pick up me some tobacco for my pipe. Do you need anything?"

"No. But I will walk with you," Nathan replies.

While in the store waiting in the line to pay for the tobacco, Nathan tells Sonny how proud he was of him to not only have made enough money to pay all his bills but to have also made enough to put some in his pocket at the end of the season. Sonny and a few others know that Big John is cheating some of the other sharecroppers out of their money. And he has been doing so for years, especially with the ones who can't read or write. Many of them know it, but they are afraid to confront him about it for fear of him throwing them off of his place or even worse.

So as Nathan gives Sonny his praise, Sonny doesn't say a word. And as they are leaving the store, one of Big John's clerks meets them at the door. "Sonny! Big John wants to see you back over at the warehouse!" the clerk says. "And if I'm not mistaken, I think it's a personal matter. So, Nathan, you can go on home," he adds as he walks past them.

Sonny tells Nathan, "Go on home, Nathan, I'll be all right."

Nathan hops on the wagon. But instead of heading home, he goes to Sonny's house to tell Mary what has happened as fast as that pair of mules can take him.

Sonny walks back into the warehouse and sees that Big John is in the middle of transacting business with one of the other sharecroppers, so he waits by the door.

After Big John is done, he calls Sonny over and says, "If you don't mind, can you hang around until I get finished settling up with the rest of these boys? I'd like to talk to you about something, private like."

"Sure, Mr. Shegogg," Sonny replies.

As the last of the sharecroppers leave the warehouse, Big John picks up his ledger books and walks upstairs to his office. After a while, he opens the door and waves his hand in the air at Sonny, letting him know that is okay from him to come up. As Sonny approaches the office, the memory of what had happened on the dark road between the cotton gin and his house some years back starts to consume his mind. And with every step that he takes toward the office, it is as if he is taking that walk home with his wife and children all over again.

Sonny starts to visualize the events of that horrible night. It is as if it was happening again at that very moment. But instead of being the victim, he is watching it as it happens. It is like an out-of-body experience.

He can hear the horses coming down the road. And as the horses come to a stop, he watches as the three men wearing hoods climb down off of them. One of the men then walks up to him and, without saying a word, hits him across the face with an ax handle. He sees himself falling to the ground.

And while he is lying on the ground, the other two men tie his hands behind his back and then pull his coveralls down to his ankles. One of the men pulls out a cotton sampling knife. Sonny sees himself screaming as they sever his testicles from his body.

The longer he reminisces about that horrible night, the angrier he becomes until he reaches the point where the anger surpasses the fear. It is as if a ton of weight has been lifted off of his shoulders. He is at a point where he doesn't give a damn if he lives or dies. All he knows is that he cannot and will not take whatever it is that Big John is about to give out any more.

As much as Sonny loves his family, he knows and understands that what he is contemplating doing will not only probably cost him his life but it will affect them as well. Yet all he can think about now is "If they try to do anything to me, someone is going to die." He then puts his hand inside of the lower pocket of his coveralls where he keeps his hook bladed knife as walks into Big Johns office.

"Go ahead and have a seat," Big John says to Sonny after he walks into the office.

"No, thank you, sir, I'd rather stand if that's all right with you," Sonny replies in a somber voice.

"The reason that I called you back in here was that I'm hearing things about you," Big John says.

"What kind of things are you hearing, Mr. Shegogg?" Sonny replies as his anger intensifies.

"Something about you wanting to move off of my place." Big John says.

Sonny doesn't say a word. He just stands there with his hand in his pocket.

"You know what I think?" Big John says as he lights up a cigar.

"What's that?" Sonny asks while staring at Big John.

"I think that you might want to rethink that," Big John says while staring back at Sonny. A bead of sweat runs down the side of Sonny's face as he starts to open the knife while keeping it in his pocket.

Just as Sonny starts to pull the knife from his pocket, there is a knock at the door. And before Big John can say come in or go away, Mary and DeEtta barge in.

"Mr. Shegogg," Mary says as she walks in and puts her arm around Sonny's waist. Big John looks at Mary and can see that she has been crying. He then looks back over at Sonny and sees a man who is truly ready to do whatever he has to do to change his present situation. Even if it means dying to do so.

After seeing that Sonny isn't going to back down. Big John says, "Sonny! Why don't you and your family go on home?" He then leans back in his chair and puffs his cigar. And as Sonny, Mary, and DeEtta walk down the steps, Big John stares at their backs as he realizes that the days of the old ways of doing business have just been numbered.

And as they walk out the door of the warehouse, Marcus is standing next to his car, waiting to give them a ride home.

CHAPTER 10

The Creek

Summer 1990—The rain bounces off of the window as Mama Dee and Jamil look out. Jamil tries to act as if he's not afraid of the thunder, but each time the lightning flashes, he moves close to Mama Dee in anticipation of the coming sound of the thunder.

"Look at the little mama's baby. He's afraid of the big bad thunder and lightning," Jazmin says after watching him from across the room.

"I thought you were watching the television," Mama Dee says to deflect the conversation away from teasing Jamil.

"I was until the TV lost its signal," Jazmin says. Another flash of lightning suddenly lights up the whole room. It is followed by another clamor of thunder that rolls across the countryside.

As the gusting wind intensifies, the power to the house abruptly goes out, and the house is submerged into a shadowy darkness just as the evening starts to fade into the night. Clarice and Stefan ramble through several of the kitchen drawers in search of candles and batteries for the flashlights.

"Is everybody okay?" Stefan asks as he continues the search for the candles and batteries.

"I think everyone is okay except for Jamil. He might have wet his pants when the lights went out," Jazmin says while laughing.

"Jazmin! Leave your brother alone!" Clarice says while holding a lit cigarette lighter for light so that Stefan can continue to look for batteries.

"Mama Dee, what did you all do back in the day when the lights went out?" Jazmin asks.

Mama Dee laughs and says, "Our lights were never on. We didn't have electricity back then."

"There was electricity back then," Jazmin says.

"I never said that there wasn't any electricity back then. I said that we didn't have any. As a matter of fact, most of the Black people who lived in the South didn't have any. And none of the ones who lived here had any. We also didn't have any indoor plumbing. That meant no indoor toilets or bathtubs.

"We cooked all of our food on a wood-burning stove and heated our houses with fireplaces or a potbelly stoves if you had the means to buy one. And when it rained like this, the sound of the raindrops hitting the tin roof is what put you to sleep at night. It also awakened you if it rained for too long. Because our fear wasn't losing power, our fear was of the creek rising and coming up out of its banks," Mama Dee explains to Jazmin. So while they all sit there in the dark, Mama Dee tells them the story about one of the times that the creek did come up out of its banks.

* * *

Early Spring 1940—"Think it's going to rain like this all night, Poppa?" Sandy Earl asks Sonny.

"Lord knows, I sure hope not," Sonny replies as they are putting on their raincoats and hats to go out and check on the livestock. As they open the door to go out, the wind blows the rain clean through to the other side of the house. Mary latches it after they exit so that the wind doesn't blow it back open while they are gone.

No sooner than Sonny and Sandy Earl get to the pasture, the lightning starts to flash. And they can see the silhouette of several of the mules on the outside of the fence. They also see another lantern off in the distance. And the person carrying it seems to be herding the mules toward their direction. As the person gets closer, Sonny shouts at him using a call that their closely-knit group uses to identify themselves to one another in the dark of night.

The shadowy figure calls back with a reply that Sonny and Sandy Earl recognize. It's Bo.

"What are you doing out here in all of this rain?" Sonny asks.

"I was checking on something and came across a couple of your mules and was running them back home to you," Bo explains.

"I sure appreciate it. We probably would have been out here half the night looking for the damn things. Do you want to come up to the house for some coffee or something to eat?" Sonny asks.

"No, I think I'm going to head on home," Bo replies.

After Sonny and Sandy Earl finish putting the mules back in their pasture, they both head back home. While walking back to the house, Sonny can't help but wonder why or what Bo was doing out in all this rain when he came across the escaped mules. He eventually lets it go after talking to Mary about it. But she too thinks it was strange, especially since it has been raining almost non-stop for two days and he lives almost on top of the hill and doesn't own any livestock.

While everyone else in the house is asleep, Sonny lies in the bed wide awake, worrying about the creek coming up out of its banks like it had done some years back. He remembers the last time that it had happened. He recalls it took out almost all the crops and many of the houses that the sharecroppers lived in at that time. The homes were lost mainly because they were built down in the low land next to the fields. The storm had happened at night, and only a few people saw it coming, and several dozen lost their lives. The families that survived it had lost almost everything they owned.

And like the beginning of a bad dream, there is a knock at the door. DeEtta gets out of her bed and goes over to answer it. It's Nathan and Jimmy.

"Hi, DeEtta, is your pa home?" Nathan asks. Just then, Sonny walks out from the bedroom, pulling his coverall straps up over his shoulders.

"Good morning, Sonny!" Nathan says.

"Good morning! What's going on?" Sonny replies.

"The bridge over the creek just got washed out, and it's starting to look like the levee is about to go. Mr. Shegogg wants every able-bodied person to head that way and help with the sandbagging."

Sonny calls out to Sandy Earl to get up and get dressed. Mary and DeEtta start to get dressed as well. "Mary, you and DeEtta stay here because if that levee breaks, the last thing that I need to be worried about is you two. So please! You two just stay here."

After getting dressed, Sonny and Sandy Earl get on the wagon with Nathan and Jimmy, and they all head off to the levee. Mary and DeEtta try to go back to bed, but all they can think about is Sonny and Sandy Earl. After lying in bed awake for several hours, they see the light of the day through the window of the bedroom. Mary, knowing that she couldn't go back to sleep even if she wanted to, gets out of bed first and starts fixing breakfast. She is soon joined by DeEtta.

While mixing the flour and water together for the biscuits, Mary starts to hum one of her songs. And as the sound of the raindrops landing on the tin roof intensifies, DeEtta goes over to the window and looks out at the water as it rushes down the ruts in the middle of the dirt road out in front of their house. There are only a few people seen moving about as the pouring slows down to a constant heavy drizzle.

When Sonny and Sandy Earl arrive at the levee, they are met with total and complete chaos. Big John and Steven are at the bridge with another crew of workers while John Jr. is in charge of the sandbagging crew there at the levee. And he doesn't have a clue about what to do or even how to do it. He tells a group of people to do one thing and then comes back a few minutes later and asks them to do something else that is completely different.

After following several of John Jr.'s chaotic instructions, Sonny tries to tell him where he should be concentrating his efforts. And just as John Jr. starts to tell him what he can do with his opinion, Sonny sees that the levee is about to be breached.

"Run!" Sonny shouts as he grabs Sandy Earl by the arm and takes off running toward one end of the twenty-eight-foot-tall levee. And as the embankment gives way, screams can be heard as the water rushes through the quickly expanding opening and carries off everyone who could not escape in time as it pours into the open cotton fields.

Back at the house, Mary tells DeEtta, "Go inside and get your raincoat and go and get some more firewood. I want to have dinner ready for your father and brother when they get home," Mary says while sitting on the front porch plucking the feathers from a chicken that she killed earlier.

"Yes, Mama," DeEtta says as she gets up and goes into the house. After getting her raincoat, she goes to the back of the house to retrieve the wood from the woodpile.

While removing logs from the woodpile, DeEtta hears a sound that she has never heard before. It is deafening and seems to be coming from a distance away. It is a snapping and grinding sound. DeEtta looks up at the skyline, and to her surprise, the face of the hill where most of the sharecroppers' shacks are located is sliding down toward the valley below.

DeEtta drops the wood and runs back to the front of the house, shouting, "Mama! The houses are sliding down the hill!"

Mary hears the screams and meets DeEtta as she turns the corner. The snapping and grinding sounds are so great that the other neighbors hear them and come running out of their houses to see what is going on.

As the front side of the hill gives way, it brings nine of the forty-three houses that dotted the hillside along with it. Screams can be heard over the sound of the snapping trees and the grinding sound of the shacks as their structure twists and pops. The people in the other shacks run down the other side of the hill carrying only a few personal items that they managed to grab and the clothes on their backs.

Mary yells out to one of the other female neighbors, "Help me hitch up the wagon!" She then tells DeEtta to go back into the house and get as many blankets and rags as she can carry. After hitching up several wagons and putting as many blankets and bandage-making materials on them as they could, the women and girls head out to help those that are caught and trapped in the massive mudslide.

"Sandy Earl! Sandy Earl! Where are you, son?" Sonny calls out as he wade through the waist-high water. He looks over at the tree line and sees several of the other workers. Some are getting out of the water, and others are pulling dead and hurting people from the water.

After making his way over to the tree line, Sonny sees John Jr. sitting on the trunk of a fallen tree. John Jr. looks up at him but doesn't say anything as he tends to his own wounds. Sonny then walks over to where the men are taking the dead bodies as they pull them from the water. As he walks past the bodies, all he can think about is how in the world he is going to tell Mary that their son is dead.

Sonny knows who each and every one of the dead is, and he thanks God that Sandy Earl isn't one of them. And as the rescuers bring over three more bodies and lay them on the ground next to the other, Sonny pulls the cover from the first one's face. And as he starts to look at the second body, he hears the word "Poppa!" He turns and sees Sandy Earl and Jimmy carrying someone who was hurt on a sheet of plywood. Sonny grabs and hugs Sandy Earl as he cries with joy. And for a moment or so, Sonny feels relieved. But as he thinks about the families of the men who lost their lives, the feeling of relief is short-lived.

"DeEtta, you stay close to me now!" Mary says as they make their way through the knee-high mud. As they pull the women and girls from the entanglement of trees and what remains of the houses, several of the ladies and girls helping with the rescue become sick and throw up from the sight of the mangled and mudded bodies. By the end of the day, they have saved eighteen people and pulled four dead bodies from the heap, and everyone else is accounted for.

The sun soon finds its way through the diminishing rain clouds and shines its rays of hope upon a hurting and demoralized people as they lay scattered out front of a row of houses with the name Shegogg painted upon their roofs. And as the rain starts to subside, their men and boys return home.

CHAPTER 11

The Reason

S ummer 1990—The next morning, Mama Dee, Jamil, and Jazmin sit out on the balcony and watch as the electrical linemen cut back the trees and reconnect the downed power lines. After a couple of hours, the power is finally restored to the house. As soon as the lights come back on, Jamil runs to tell Clarice and Stefan, who are still in their bedroom asleep.

After the electrical trucks and crews are gone, Mama Dee asks, "Who wants breakfast?"

Jazmin and Jamil simultaneously answer, "I do!" as they jump to their feet and run downstairs to the kitchen. Mama Dee takes her time getting up and takes the elevator down to join them. By the time she gets there, Jazmin and Jamil have already pulled the eggs and bacon from the refrigerator.

The smell of the eggs and bacon cooking in the skillet fills the house as Mama Dee works her magic in the kitchen.

"What's on the menu?" Clarice asks as she and Stefan walk into the kitchen, heading straight for the pot coffee that Mama Dee has made.

"Eggs and bacon!" Jamil replies.

After getting his coffee, Stefan sits down at the table, and Mama Dee sits a plate of food down in front of him. At first, Stefan tries to pretend that he didn't notice it being there. But it only takes a moment or so for the aroma of the bacon to get the best of him. And before he knows it, he has consumed every crumb.

"Thanks for breakfast, Mama," Stefan says as he takes a sip of his coffee before getting up from the table.

"You are welcome, son," Mama Dee replies. After everyone has finished eating, Jazmin stays behind to help Mama Dee clean up the kitchen.

While loading the dishwasher, Jazmin asks, "Mama Dee, what happened after the levee broke and the mudslide?"

Mama Dee then picks up where she left off at telling the story.

* * *

Early Spring 1940—Once the rains had stopped, it was time to bury the dead. Nine men and boys had lost their lives at the levee, and four women and girls had lost theirs in the mudslide. It was not as bad as the previous time that the creek had risen up out of its banks. But still, over 80 percent of the cotton crops were lost along with half of the livestock. And Mr. Shegogg used the tragedy to increase the debt of the sharecroppers who had survived and had no place else to go.

During the funerals, Rev. Mitchel preached a lot about God doing things for a reason. But DeEtta could never figure out exactly what the reason for the levee giving way and the mudslide was.

"Mama, if Rev. Mitchel says that it was 'God's will' that made these bad things happen one more time, I'm going to change churches," DeEtta says as they rode to church in the used pickup truck Sonny recently bought with some of the money that they had been saving to buy a house with.

"Girl, please. You ought to know by now that Rev. Mitchel only has so many sermons memorized. And he has had to bury more people this week than he has buried in the last ten years. So give him a break…please. For me," Mary replies.

As they pull up in front of the church, they see Marcus standing out front waiting on DeEtta so that they can go in together and sit next to one another.

"Good morning, Marcus," Mary says as she and Sonny walk past him.

"Good morning, Mr. and Mrs. Wells," Marcus says as he and DeEtta file in behind them. Marcus whispers something to DeEtta, and she whispers something back to him before walking into the church. As the funeral begins, Rev. Mitchel asks for a donation to help the families out with the cost of the burials.

Mary whispers something into Sonny's ear. Sonny then signals for one of the ushers to come over. Mary hands the usher a note and tells him to take it to Rev. Mitchel. After receiving the note and reading it, Rev. Mitchel says, "God is *good*! An anonymous member of our congregation has paid for the burial in full. It is incredible how quick the Lord can work sometimes. You see, everything happens for a reason…" As he continues on with one of his "everything happens for a reason" sermons, DeEtta taps her mother on her shoulder. And as Mary turns and looks at her, she shakes her head.

Later that evening DeEtta and Marcus sits on his front porch talking.

"Now that they have buried Mrs. Wilson, maybe things will start getting back to normal around here, being that she was last one to be buried. At the funeral I couldn't help thinking about her husband and children. *What are they going to do now that she is no longer here?*" DeEtta says.

DeEtta then gets up and walks over behind where Marcus is sitting and puts her arms around his neck and bends down and kisses him on the top of his head.

"I hope so too. And to keep from getting too sad, I try to think about things like, 'How blessed they were to have someone like her in their lives.' You know, some people live a life time and never have anyone in their life that will make a big enough difference to even be missed." Marcus replies as he rubs DeEtta's arms.

"Its starting to get late. I think that I need to head home." DeEtta says

"I'll drive you." Marcus says as he stands and turns to face her.

"I think that the walk will help me clear my head." DeEtta say.

Marcus takes DeEtta by her arms and pulls her in close. He then looks her in the eyes and says, "DeEtta, I've been trying to figure out a way and a right time to ask you something. But with the funerals and all of the other stuff. It never seemed like there was a right time. So…I'm going to just ask it. DeEtta, will you marry me?"

DeEtta's without hesitation answers with a tearful, "Yes!" as they hug and kiss.

The following Sunday after church, DeEtta tells her mother that Marcus will be taking her home and that he had something to ask her and Poppa when they get there. Mary had a good idea of what he was about to ask them. Yet she didn't say a word about it to Sonny because she wasn't quite sure of how he was going to react. As Sonny pulls the truck onto the side of the house, he sees Marcus and DeEtta standing on the porch.

As he and Mary get out of the truck, Marcus and DeEtta walk up to the truck, and Marcus takes off his hat and starts to fidget around with it as if he's nervous.

"What's wrong with you, boy? You look as if you are constipated or something," Sonny says as he walks past them.

Mary stops and says, "Sonny, I think he has something to ask you."

Sonny stops and turns and looks at Marcus. And from the look in Marcus's eyes, Sonny knows exactly what he was about to ask him.

Marcus then says, "Mr. and Mrs. Wells, I have known you all for pretty much my whole life. And your family and my family have seen and shared a lot of good and bad times together. And the breaking of the levee and the washing out of the bridge made me—"

"Come on, son, get to the point! Or are you planning on jaw jacking all evening?" Sonny says as he interrupts him. Mary nudges Sonny and tells him to shut up and let the boy speak.

Marcus then continues, "Well sir...*and* ma'am, what I'm trying to say is—"

Sonny then interrupts again and says, "Don't try! Say!" Mary nudges him again and smiles.

"Can DeEtta and I get married?" Marcus blurs out.

At first, Sonny doesn't say a word. He just looks over at DeEtta as she bubbles with joy in her anticipation that he and Mary will give their blessing. Sonny then looks back over at Marcus and asks, "How are you intending on taking care of my daughter if I was to give my blessing?"

"By working hard just like you and my father do, sir!" Marcus replies.

Sonny looks at Mary and sees that she is as excited about it as DeEtta is. After seeing the look on Mary's face, he gives his blessing. He then invites Marcus into the house to have a drink of moonshine to celebrate while Mary and DeEtta go into the bedroom to talk about the wedding plans.

Marcus and Sonny sip on moonshine well into the night, stopping only after Sonny passes out. Marcus then staggers down the road and up the hill home, leaving his car parked in front of DeEtta's house.

The next morning when Marcus returns to get his car, he knocks on the door, and no one answers. After seeing that truck is gone, he assumes that they are all gone as well. And as he gets into his car to leave, Jimmy comes walking down the road from up the hill.

"How is it going, Marcus?" Jimmy asks.

"It's going pretty good right about now," Marcus replies.

"I asked DeEtta parents for her hand in marriage yesterday," Marcus tells him with a smile on his face.

Jimmy knows what the answer must have been. "I guess congratulations are in order," Jimmy says with a grin.

"Yes, sir, it is!" Marcus replies. Marcus then asks Jimmy, "Where are you headed to?"

"I'm on my way to town. But first, I was going to stop by and see Sara," he answers.

"Do you need a ride?" Marcus asks.

"Sure!" he replies. They both then get into Marcus's car and take off toward Sara's house.

While riding along, Marcus asks Jimmy, "So when are you going to ask Sara to marry you? You know that she's not going to wait around forever. Especially after she finds out that DeEtta's getting married."

They both laugh and Jimmy shakes his head in agreement. "So when is the big day?" Jimmy asks.

"We really haven't had time to pick one yet. But I was thinking sometime after the first of the year. That way I'll have some time to save up some money and find us a place to live. But you know how women are. If I say after the first of the year, she will probably say, 'Let's do it tomorrow,'" Marcus concludes.

As they pull up to Sara's house, they see her and DeEtta standing out front talking.

"I think you better get ready to be pressured into getting married. See the looks on their faces?" Marcus says to Jimmy after stopping the car.

"How you doing there, bride-to-be?" Jimmy asks as he gets out of the car.

"I'm doing fine. But the bride-to-be part is not quite official yet, being that I haven't been properly asked yet," DeEtta says while smiling at Marcus.

Marcus gets out of the car and walks over to her and says, "You know, you're right. I haven't properly asked you yet." Marcus then pulls a ring from his pocket and gets down on one knee. "I was going to do this yesterday, but your father got me all mixed up and nervous. Then I was going to do it the first thing this morning. But everybody was gone when I got to your house. So I'm going to do it right now. DeEtta Wells, I love you more then I love life itself. You are the first thing that I think about in the morning and the last thing that I think about at night. The sight of you heals my soul after a long hard day in the fields, and your touch is what calms me when I'm upset. You are truly heaven-sent for me. Will you do me the honor of becoming my wife?" Marcus then places the engagement ring on her finger.

By the time Marcus finishes, both DeEtta and Sara are in tears. Jimmy gets so caught up in the moment that he then gets down on one knee and proposes to Sara. Sara answers before he can get it all out of his mouth. She and DeEtta then run into her house to tell her parents, leaving Marcus and Jimmy standing outside next to Marcus's car looking at one another with a sort of "I wonder what's next?" look on their faces.

It didn't take long for the word to spread. Before the week is out, everyone who lives on the old plantation is talking about DeEtta and Sara getting married.

"I am so happy for both of you," Julia says as she, DeEtta, and Sara walk down the road on their way back from picking beans from the field to cook for dinner the coming Sunday.

"Thanks, Julia! And you do know that you got to be in both of our weddings?" Sara says.

As they walk past DeEtta's house, Sara says her good-byes and continues on up the hill toward her house. After Sara has walked off, Julia asks DeEtta, "Would it be okay if I stop by your house and rest for a bit before heading home?"

"Sure! Come on in, and we can get started on snapping these beans while you rest," DeEtta replies.

DeEtta then goes inside to get a couple of big pans while Julia takes a seat in one of the chairs on the porch. After returning, DeEtta sits down next to her and gives her one of the pans. While snapping the beans, DeEtta starts to hums a song without even realizing that she is doing it.

"What are you humming?" Julia asks.

"Oh…nothing," DeEtta replies.

"DeEtta, if I told you something, would you promise to keep it between us?" Julia asks as she seems to have moved from having a general conversation to a more serious one.

"Why, yes. You are my best friend, and I promise to take it to the grave with me. Now, what's on your mind?" DeEtta asks.

"Well…I have a friend." Julia says.

"Julia! You have a lot of friends. Me being one of them," DeEtta replies.

"I'm talking about a male friend, DeEtta," Julia explains.

"Okay, good for you. What's his name?" DeEtta asks.

"That's the problem. Mama and Poppa would just die if they knew who he was," Julia says.

And just as Julia is about to tell DeEtta the name of her newly found love, Mary walks out onto the porch. "How are the beans coming?" Mary asks.

"They are coming along just great, Mama," DeEtta answers.

Mary pulls up a chair and starts giving them a hand with the beans. After finishing, Julia puts hers in a burlap sack and heads home.

CHAPTER 12

Willie Lee

Summer 1990—"Why don't you park that thing and help them unload that stuff from that truck?" Mama Dee says to Jamil as he sits on the golf cart, watching the men from the nursery unload the plants, mulch, and potting soil that Stefan ordered for her.

"They are getting paid to do that, Mama Dee. And besides, Daddy told me to stay out of their way."

Mama Dee shakes her head and mumbles to herself, "That is why these kids are so lazy! Nobody makes them do anything!" She walks over to count the number of plants.

Stefan doesn't say a word. He just continues to sit on the porch and act as if he is reading a book. After the men are done unloading, Stefan puts down the book, gets up, and goes over to sign the delivery receipt. "Jamil! Bring that cart over here." Stefan says. "I want you to help Mama Dee plant her flowers. She is not to lift anything! Do you understand?" Stefan says while giving Jamil a very stern look.

"Yes, Sir!" Jamil replies.

Mama Dee smiles because she sees this as progress—Stefan finally making the boy do something other than half clean his room.

"And if you do a good job, there might be something in it for you," Stefan adds. Mama Dee then shakes her head again as Stefan looks at her and hunches his shoulder and asks, "What's wrong with that?"

Jamil loads several of the bags of potting soil and a few trays of the plants onto the back of the cart. Mama Dee then climbs into the front seat, and they both head around to the backside of the house. After unloading the soil and plants. Mama Dee tells Jamil to pour one of the bags of potting soil into a large flower pot that is sitting next to the back door of the house. After Jamil is done filling the first pot with soil, she tells him to fill the pot on the other side of the back door with the same amount of soil while she plants some of the flowers in the first pot.

After repeating the process for about an hour and a half, moving from flower pot to flower pot around the large house, Jamil breaks his self-imposed silence, "Mama Dee? Why are you always trying to do some work?" he asks.

At first, Mama Dee isn't sure how to respond. But after giving it a bit of thought, she says, "If you never do anything, you will never know how to do anything. And if you don't know how to do anything, how will you ever take care of yourself when your parents are no longer around to do it?"

After giving her answer some thought, Jamil then asks, "Was there ever a time when you didn't like to work?"

Mama Dee answers, "You know…there probably was, but I don't remember. Because when I was eight years old, my brother and I would go to the cotton field with Mama and Poppa. We had to pull our weight too, you know. Especially my brother Sandy Earl. By the time he was fourteen years old, he could pick almost as much cotton as Poppa."

Jamil then asks, "Did Uncle Sandy Earl ever want to just hang out with his friends and do nothing?"

Mama Dee doesn't reply; she just pauses as she recalls a name. The name was that of a boy she knew when she was growing up. This boy's name was Willie Lee, and he loved to hang out with his friends sometimes and just do nothing.

*　*　*

Fall 1940—DeEtta and Mary both wake up early that morning—Mary because she had to make Sonny and Sandy Earl's breakfast before they head off to the fields and DeEtta because she is so excited about her upcoming wedding even though it's months away.

"Mama, what colors should I do for my wedding?" DeEtta asks while using the rim of the top to a mason jar to cut out the dough for the biscuits.

"I don't know. I think that is a decision that you and Marcus should be making together," Mary answers. "And besides, if you two are going to wait until the spring to get married, you have plenty of time to decide," Mary adds. Just then, there is a knock at the door. Sonny is in the front room shaving, so he answers it. It's Bo.

87

"Good morning, Sonny. How is the family?" Bo asks.

"Everyone is doing fine. What brings you by here this early?" Sonny asks.

"Well…when I was uptown this morning, I ran into Sam Brown and a few other guys that live on Mr. Shaw's place. They're looking for Sam's nephew. He has been missing for about three days now. And the last time that anybody saw him was Friday night walking down Old Mason Road heading home," Bo says.

"Which one of those boys is Sam's nephew? I remember seeing three or four of them from the Shaw's place hanging out together all the time. But I don't quite remember which ones belonged to what family," Sonny asks.

"He was the tall one who always wore the coverall with the one strap dangling. I believe his name is Willie Lee," Bo says.

"I'll ask around," Sonny says.

Bo then tells Sonny goodbye and gets in his truck and leaves for home.

Sonny goes back into the house where Mary is still busy cooking breakfast. "What did Bo want?" Mary asks.

"He asked me if I've seen Sam Brown's nephew. He's been missing since last Friday." Sonny says.

"Are you talking about Willie Lee?" Sandy Earl asks.

"I believe that's who he said it was," Sonny says.

"I know him! He's tall and about eighteen years old. He probably took off and headed for the city," Sandy Earl says.

"What makes you say that, Sandy Earl?" Sonny asks.

"Because I saw him hanging around with some of the guys who work over at the cotton gin. They were talking about the car plants in Detroit and Milwaukie that are hiring," Sandy Earl says.

"I sure hope so. That's a good thing if he had enough sense to get away from here," Sonny replies.

After finishing breakfast, they both head off to work. Once they make it to the fields, Sonny climbs onto the old tractor that he bought on credit from the tractor dealer uptown to replace his team of mules. As he works on getting the tractor started, he tells Sandy Earl to take the truck and go to the depot and get a full load of manure so that he can mix it in with the soil as he plows under the cotton plant stalks.

The depot is only a few miles away, so it doesn't take Sandy Earl long to get there. As he pulls the truck up to the loading area, he sees Marcus loading spools of baling wire onto a truck. Marcus is one of the lucky ones because he was able to get a job at the depot, which is owned by Mr. Baum. Mr. Baum is a rich businessman from up north who own depots all over the South. He lives in New York City and only comes down just before the Christmas holidays to personally pass out turkeys to all of his employees even though he is Jewish and Christmas is not a holiday that he and his family celebrates.

The head manager at this particular depot is one of Mr. Baum's relatives, and he is from up north as well and isn't that bad a person to work for. But Marcus's direct supervisor is from Cleveland, Mississippi, and he is as mean as a snake. His name is Tommy. He and John Jr.

are good friends and often hang out and drink together along with several of their other friends.

"Marcus! Grab a couple of shelves and help him load his pickup truck with manure when you get done loading that wire," Tommy tells Marcus.

After finishing loading the wire, Marcus hops into the truck with Sandy Earl, and they drive around back to where the manure and compost is kept. While shoveling the fertilizer into the bed of the pickup truck, Sonny Earl and Marcus talk about the missing boy.

"I hear everybody is looking for Willie Lee," Marcus says.

"Yeah, I heard. But I think he ran off to Detroit because the other day some of the guys were talking about the car plants up there hiring. And I saw him listening with both ears wide open," Sandy Earl says with a chuckle. "And if that's true, I say, 'Well, good for him.' I've been thinking about getting the hell away from here myself. If it wasn't for Mama and Papa, I'd been gone a long time ago," Sandy Earl adds as they finish loading the truck. After telling Marcus that he will see him later, Sandy Earl heads back to the field, and Marcus goes back inside to find Tommy to tell him that he is done with the loading.

Later that day, Sara stops by DeEtta's house to talk about their weddings. "I've been hearing some things about our friend Julia," Sara says shortly after getting there.

"What kind of things are you hearing?" DeEtta asks.

"Well…I was told by a very reliable source that they saw her leaving the Shegogg's house through the back door late Thursday night," Sara says.

"Okay…she left the Shegoggs' house late one night. Maybe she was cleaning their house for them or something? And unless something has recently changed that I haven't heard about, every Negro leaves that house through the back door," DeEtta replies. "And, unless my memory is failing me, I think darn near all of us have cleaned their house at one time or another to make some extra money," DeEtta adds. She then asks, "What did you come by here for anyway? Just to gossip? Or to make plans for our weddings?"

Sara's face lights up with a huge smile when DeEtta pulls out a book full of pictures of wedding gowns that she got from Mrs. Loo. While looking through the book and doing a lot of going back and forth, Sara decides that she will have her wedding in the coming spring. And DeEtta decides to have hers in the early summer. That way, all of their friends will be able to attend both of their weddings.

Before long, the sun starts to set in the sky as the evening approaches. Sara then says her goodbyes and heads off for home. Not long after Sara leaves, Marcus stops by after getting off work.

"Good evening, Mrs. Wells," Marcus says as he speaks to Mary, who is sitting out on the front porch with DeEtta. Mary returns the pleasantry before going into the house to set the table for dinner.

While Marcus and DeEtta sit on the porch talking, Sonny and Sandy Earl return home from the field.

"I guess now that you and DeEtta are getting married, I'm going to be seeing a lot more of you. Aren't I?" Sonny asks as he steps onto the porch.

After a brief hesitation to try and figure out what would be the correct answer, Marcus answers, "Yes…sir?"

DeEtta and Sandy Earl laugh, but Sonny doesn't reply to Marcus's answer. He just continues walking into the house.

"I don't think that your father cares that much for me," Marcus says after the screen door slams shut.

"He likes you. That's why he messes with you so much," DeEtta explains.

Sandy Earl then jokingly says, "Yep! Pops was just telling me today while we were working in the field, 'That boy Marcus is going to make me the proudest father-in-law on this here place.'"

They all laugh as Sandy Earl heads on into the house to wash up for dinner.

"Marcus, would you like to stay for dinner? We have plenty," Mary asks as she opens the screen door and sticks her head out.

"Yes, ma'am, I would love that," Marcus replies with a grin on his face.

"After dinner, you can give me another driving lesson in your car," DeEtta adds.

During dinner, most of the conversation is about Marcus and DeEtta's upcoming wedding, which means that Mary and DeEtta are doing most of the talking. After they are done eating, Marcus and DeEtta go outside and get into Marcus's car. DeEtta gets in behind the wheel, and Marcus climbs in on the passenger side. After reminding DeEtta of how everything operates and where the gas pedal, clutch, and brakes are at, they are ready for her second driver's lesson.

The neighbors point as they see DeEtta drive down the road for the first time. And some even laugh as they watch the car jerk and sputter as she steps on the clutch and grinds on its gears as she shifts it into gear. All that sputtering and grinding doesn't deter DeEtta one bit because she is determined to learn how to drive.

The longer she drives, the better she becomes. And by the time the moon has risen high in the night sky, DeEtta is handling Marcus's old Ford like she has been driving it her whole life. After making it back to her house, DeEtta pleads with Marcus to let her drop him off at work tomorrow morning and that he let her keep the car so that she and Sara can go to the Chinamen store to look at wedding stuff. "I promise to be very careful and to be outside waiting when you get off work," DeEtta says. Marcus reluctantly agrees.

The next morning, Marcus arrives at DeEtta's house early. Sonny notices that DeEtta is up and dressed before he and Sandy Earl are out of bed.

"Why are you up and dressed so early this morning?" Sonny asks DeEtta.

"I'm dropping Marcus off at work today," DeEtta replies.

Sonny walks over to the window and looks out and sees Marcus sitting in the car, waiting. He then shakes his head in disbelief as he says, "I can't believe that he is going to let you have that car. You've only been driving a day for heaven's sake." As Sonny and Sandy Earl are leaving for work, Sonny walks up next to the truck where Sandy Earl is standing.

"Good morning, Mr. Wells," Marcus says.

Sonny looks at him and asks, "Are you really going to let her drive that car?"

"Well sir ah…" Marcus replies.

Sonny doesn't say another word; he just shakes his head from side to side once more as he walks off. He then gets into his truck with Sandy Earl and drives off.

DeEtta comes out of the house shortly after and walks over to the driver's side of the car and motions for Marcus to slide over to the passenger's side. After getting behind the wheel, she gives Marcus a kiss on the lips and tells him how much she loves him. She then starts the car, eases out onto the street, and takes off flying down the road, leaving a large plume of dust behind her.

After dropping Marcus off, DeEtta goes back home and gives her mother a hand cleaning the kitchen while she waits for the stores uptown to open. After finishing the kitchen and completing a few other chores around the house, she heads out to pick up Julia and Sara. As DeEtta drives up, she sees Sara walking out of her door. Sara looks over at the car. And then looks again.

"Oh my God! Look who's driving!" she says as she breaks into her happy dance and runs over and hops into the passenger side of the car.

DeEtta is smiling from ear to ear as they drive off to go and pick up Julia. After parking the car in front of Julia's house, DeEtta asks Sara to go up and knock on the door. Shortly after Sara knocks on the door, Julia answers it. After opening the door, Julia starts to talk to Sara but after glancing over and seeing Marcus's car, she asks, "Where is DeEtta? And why are you riding around with Marcus without her?" Sara laughs and tells Julia to take a closer look at the driver.

After seeing DeEtta behind the wheel, Julia breaks out into her happy dance and then rushes out to the car bare-footed, wearing nothing but a housecoat and panties. After a jubilant conversation, Julia runs back into the house and gets dressed, and the three of them head down the road toward town.

As they are driving down the dusty road, their child-ish conversations of old are no more. Instead, these have been replaced with the things that mature women talk about. It is as if maturity and adulthood have somehow crept up from behind them without them knowing and removed all of the mannerisms, thoughts, and wants that consume the mind of an adolescent and left behind the desires, ideas, and burdens of adulthood. They have become women.

While driving through the center of town, they come upon an older Black man in a wagon being pulled by a couple of mules. Seeing the man with the wagon and mules reminds DeEtta of how far they have come since they all were little children. She can imagine them not too long ago riding in the back of a wagon not too dif-ferent than the one that he is driving.

And as the wagon turns off the road and goes into the parking lot of the Shegogg's family store, the girls see Steven Shegogg standing out front. Steven, thinking that it is Marcus who is driving, waves at the car as it passes.

After making it to their destination, DeEtta parks in the back of Mr. Loo's store instead of out front since her parallel parking skills are nonexistent. While walking around to the front of the store to enter, they hear the squeal of car tires. It's John Jr. and one of his friends racing their cars through the middle of town.

Sheriff Pickens and one of his deputies hop in their car as if they were going to go chasing behind them. But by the time they get into their car and get it started, John Jr. is long gone. And besides, everyone in town, including Sheriff Pickens and his deputies, know not only who they are but that if they did catch them, nothing would happen.

No sooner have the girls walked into the store than they are greeted by Mrs. and Mr. Loo.

"How is your mother doing?" Mrs. Loo asks DeEtta.

"She is doing well," DeEtta replies.

"So what brings you into the store today?" Mrs. Loo asks.

DeEtta then tells her about her and Marcus's plans to get married. And after Mrs. Loo starts to congratulate her, DeEtta says, "Sara is getting married as well."

Mrs. Loo and her husband don't really know Sara and her family all that well although Sara's father worked in the fields as hard as Sonny did. They hardly ever had any extra money because he would either drink it up in moonshine or allow Big John to cheat him out of it. Either way, it left Sara and her mother with little to make do with.

"We would like to see some of those bridal catalogs that you have. Like the one you gave me a few weeks ago," DeEtta asks.

Mrs. Loo smiles as she goes into the back room. A short time later, she returns with a box full of magazines and catalogs. Some were old, and the others were very old. "These are not the latest, but they will give you some ideas of what you might want. And as the wedding day gets closer, I will order a new catalog, and you ladies can pick out what you want from it," Mrs. Loo explains.

DeEtta thanks Mrs. Loo as they leave with the box of magazines. After putting the box on the backseat, Julia says, "I think that I'll walk back to the house."

"Walk back? That's a three-mile walk," Sara replies.

"That's if you take the shortcut near the cemetery. If you stay on the road, it's almost seven miles," DeEtta adds.

After going back and forth for a while, Sara and DeEtta decide to let it go. And as they drive off, Julia waves to them while standing in front of Mr. Loo's store. DeEtta and Sara talk and think about Julia all the way home.

"You know, I just put myself in her place. And if my two best friends were about to get married and I wasn't. Well...I think that it would make me feel some kind of way too," Sara says.

"You just might have something there, Sara," DeEtta says while thinking about the conversation that she and Julia had had on her porch the day that her mother interrupted their conversation. DeEtta drops Sara off at her house with half of the magazines and catalogs and heads to Marcus's job to wait for him to get off.

Julia looks through the windows of the stores as she walks past them. And as she passes the Shegogg's store, Steven sees her and waves. Not wanting anyone to think that something is going on between them, Julia just nods her head in acknowledgment as she continues on her way.

As she reaches the outskirts of town, Julia veers off the road to take the shortcut. This was the route that the sharecroppers took back when they would ride to town together on the wagon pulled by the mules. The path is now somewhat overgrown and seldom used much anymore. After walking the path for only a short while, she hears someone yell out from behind her, "Wait up!"

It is Steven. Julia stops and waits.

"How are you doing?" Steven asks.

"I'm doing okay, I guess," Julia replies as they both walk down the path together. "You do know that you are going to get me and you killed if anyone sees us together and thinks that we're dating or something. Don't you?" Julia says.

"You know Julia, the way I feel about you, I couldn't give a damn about what they think," Steven says as he takes her by the hand. "What do you think about me and you running off to California and getting married? We would never ever have to come back here," Steven says.

Julia laughs as she keeps on walking. Steven then takes her by the hand once more, stops, and kneels down on one knee.

"*No!* Don't do that. I can't leave. What would my family think of me?" Julia asks as she pulls away and starts to run off while crying and confused about her feelings for Steven.

She suddenly stops and stares at a large shadow that is up in the trees. And as the wind changes its direction, her nostrils confirm what her eyes are seeing. It is Willie

Lee's partly charred body. He has been hung by his neck and is dangling about three feet off of the ground. A pile of ashes is all that remains of the wood that was used to fuel the fire beneath him.

Julia and Steven stand petrified before Willie Lee's rotting corpse. They can't help but think about how he was once a living, breathing, and loving human being. And now he is neither living nor breathing. Julia feels as if the whole world has seemingly stopped in the middle of its rotation.

CHAPTER 13

The Revenuers

Summer 1990—After working in the yard for two straight days, Mama Dee and Jamil finally finish planting all the flowers that Stefan had bought. And Jamil can't wait until his father gets home from work so that he can receive whatever it was that Stefan had promised to give him.

"So what are you going to buy with the money that your father promised you?" Mama Dee asks.

"Not sure. But with school starting in about eight weeks, I've been thinking about getting me a pair of those new Jordan's. Maybe the ones with the red trim," Jamil answers. "Mama Dee, with all the bad stuff that was going on down here when you were young, why did you all stay?" Jamil asks as he reflects back on some of the stories that she told him while planting the flowers.

"We would have if we had a place to go. You see, just when my parents were beginning to see a little prosperity from all their years of labor, the Depression hit, and boy, did it hit us Black people hard! Especially down here in the South. It took pretty much everything they

100

could muster to keep from starving to death," Mama Dee explains.

"Jamil! Go wash up for dinner and stop asking your grandmother so many questions," Clarice says shortly after coming out of the house to see the flowers that they had planted.

"His questions don't bother me, Clarice. I truly love the fact that my grandchildren don't mind being around me. I was talking to Sara on the phone just the other day, and she said that her grandchildren don't have anything to do with her unless she is giving them something. So! Like I said, I love the fact that they like being around me," Mama Dee says as she heads into the house as well to get ready for dinner.

After dinner, Clarice makes Jazmin and Jamil put the dishes in the dishwasher while she and Mama Dee pick out a movie for them all to watch on the television. "What do you want to watch tonight, Mama Dee?" Clarice asks.

"Whatever you want to watch. I'm not that particular," Mama Dee replies.

Jazmin and Jamil joined their mother and Mama Dee in the family room after finishing putting the dishes in the dishwasher. No sooner do they walk into the room than they start to arguing over what to watch on the television. Jazmin wants to watch some love story, and Jamil wants to watch the basketball game. After telling them to stop arguing several times without either one shutting their mouths, Clarice sends them both up to their rooms.

As they go stomping off to their rooms, Clarice looks over at Mama Dee and sees the look on her face, and asks, "What?"

After clearing her throat, Mama Dee says, "If my mother had to tell me to shut up more than once, I would have been so sore that I wouldn't have been able to sit down for a month of Sundays. And I know what you are thinking right now. That was back then, and this is now. But Clarice, if you don't run them, they are going to run you. And that is all I'm going to say about that," Mama Dee adds. Clarice loudly exhales and doesn't say anything more about it.

While scanning through the channels on the television, they come across an old black-and-white movie about some Chicago gangsters trying to take a bunch moonshine from the hillbillies who made it.

"This was back in your days, wasn't it, Mama Dee?" Clarice jokingly says.

Mama Dee smiles as she continues to watch the movie. In one scene in the movie, the revenue officer knocks on the hillbillies' door. That scene reminds Mama Dee of something that happened when she was younger. She shares the memory with Clarice.

* * *

Fall 1940—As the day comes to an end, Sonny heads toward the shed with the tractor. While he is driving along the edge of the freshly turned field, the dust kicked up by the tractor tires rises up into the air and is carried off by the gusting winds as they roll across the open field's dry and loosened soil. The aroma of the newly laid manure that Sonny has just finished spreading is very prevalent in the air.

Sandy Earl opens the door of the shed when he sees that Sonny is heading in his direction. After opening the door, he picks up all of the tools that they had used during the day and takes them inside and puts them away. Sonny drives the tractor straight into the shed and turns it off.

"We did good today, son. The fields are ready for next season planting," Sonny says as he puts his hand on Sandy Earl's shoulder while walking toward the truck. As they walk up to the truck, Sandy Earl takes the dipper from the bucket of water sitting on the lowered tailgate and offers it to his father. "Go ahead, son, you go first. As hard as you worked today, you earned it," Sonny says.

After taking a drink, Sandy Earl gives the dipper to his father, walks around to the other side of the truck, and starts taking off his boots to prepare for the ride home. Sonny sticks the dipper into the bucket of water and scoops up some. As he drinks it down, he notices that someone is moving in the woods. They are just inside of the tree line. At first, Sonny starts to say something to Sandy Earl. Then he recognizes who it is. It's Bo.

Sonny acts as if he doesn't notice him watching them. And while still keeping an eye on him, Sonny changes his boots as well. He and Sandy Earl then climb into the truck and head for home.

As they are driving off, Sonny looks in the review mirror and sees Bo as he walks out of the woods and onto the trail carrying a large sack. As Sonny continues to drive, he wonders, *what it is that Bo is doing that is so secret that he feels that he has to hide it from them.*

Once they make it home, Sonny allows Sandy Earl to take his bath first because he knows that he wants to catch up with his friends before it gets too late.

While they are both carrying buckets of water to fill the tub, Sandy Earl asks his father, "Did you see Mr. Bo standing over in the tree line today?"

At first, Sonny isn't sure of what to say because he didn't think that Sandy Earl had seen him. After giving it a bit of thought, Sonny replies, "Yes, I did."

Sandy Earl then says, "I usually only see him out there about once a week. But that makes the third time that I have seen him this week."

"Do you have any idea of what it is that he is doing?" Sonny asks.

"No, I don't, Pa," Sandy Earl replies.

After taking his bath, Sandy Earl quickly gets dressed and helps his father refill the tub before leaving to be with his friends. As Sonny soaks in the tub, Mary washes his back.

"I saw the strangest thing today," Sonny says.

"What was that?" Mary asks.

"While working in the field today, I saw Bo standing in the woods as if he was trying to hide from Sandy Earl and me," Sonny says.

"Did you say anything to him?" Mary asks.

"No, I pretended like I didn't see him. Sandy Earl told me just a little while ago that he sees him hiding out there all the time," Sonny answers.

"What do you think it is that he is doing?" Mary asks.

"I really have no idea," Sonny answers as he takes a sip from the cup of moonshine that Mary has poured for him to help him relax.

The following day is a Saturday. And Saturday is the day that Sonny takes Mary to town and do her shopping for the week. As they pull up to the grocery store, they notice some commotion over at the sheriff's office. It is Rev. Mitchel along with a group of people from their congregation. They are protesting the way that Sheriff Pickens is handling the investigation into Willie Lee's murder. Sonny tells Mary to go on into the store and get what she needs while he goes over to see what is going on.

"Sheriff Pickens, sir! I know that you are a busy man. But surely you can spend more time than you and your deputies have to try and find the people who killed this young man!" Rev. Mitchel asks.

A couple of the deputies are standing inside, looking out of the window. They are joking and smiling as if they are watching a sideshow of some sort.

Willie Lee's uncle and mother are standing in the front of the crowd, and the mother is noticeably upset. John Jr., along with a bunch of his friends, are sitting across the street on the lot of his father's store. They're entertaining themselves by drinking beer and yelling obscenities at Rev. Mitchel and his congregation.

"Now, you all need to go on home and let the law handle this," Sheriff Pickens says as he steps down off of the porch and walks over toward Rev. Mitchel. Sonny walks over and stands behind the reverend so that he can better hear what is being said.

"There are all kinds of evidence, like beer cans, balled-up cigarette packs, and only God knows what else you or your deputies never bothered to collect," the reverend says. "Truly! This family deserves some justice," Rev. Mitchell proclaims.

Sonny can see that Sheriff Pickens is starting to get angry. So he takes Rev. Mitchel by the arm and pulls him back into the crowd so that it is not like the reverend is the only one confronting the sheriff. The sheriff then signals for his deputies to come out of the office. As they exit the office, one grabs a rather long nightstick and the other a shotgun.

As the reverend reiterates his call for justice, the two deputies step down off the porch and walk toward the crowd.

"Mr. Sheriff! Justice may be optional for some to give and others to receive in this life. But in the next life, it is a prerequisite to entering into the kingdom of heaven. So I ask you again. Please give this family justice," the reverend says.

Sheriff Pickens then leans in close to the reverend and says, "I guess you'll be getting your justice in the next life. Now! You and your band of niggers, get y'all asses in y'all's vehicles and on them damn mules and get the hell off my streets before my deputies and I commence to whipping ass and taking names. And that includes you two!" he adds as he points his finger at Willie Lee's mother and uncle.

The reverend looks back at his congregation, which consists of mostly very young and elderly people. He then realizes that, at this time, their powers are limited.

So he instructs them to go home. Sonny walks back over to the grocery store and waits by his truck for Mary to finish shopping.

While driving home, Sonny tells Mary about what had gone on in front of the sheriff's office and what Sheriff Pickens had told the reverend.

"What did they expect? Justice for the lynching of a Black boy by a bunch of Klan members here in Mississippi?" Mary sarcastically asks. "And I just know that John Jr. had something to do with it. I would bet my last dollar on that," Mary says as she continues to vent.

After making it back to the house, Sonny waits on the front porch for Sandy Earl and DeEtta to get home. About an hour later, Sandy Earl comes walking down the road. Marcus drops DeEtta off about ten minutes later.

"I need to talk to you two," Sonny says. DeEtta sits down on the steps, and Sandy Earl leans against the post. Marcus starts to walk back over to his car to leave but is stopped by Sonny saying, "You going to be family soon enough, so you need to hear this too."

Sonny and Mary sit down next to each other in the rocking chairs.

"I just witnessed something uptown that really upset your mother and me," Sonny says. He then goes on to tell them about what had happened. "I don't want you all going anywhere by yourself or staying out late without us knowing where you are. And for God's sake! Never walk these roads unless there are at least four or five of y'all together in a group. And stay the hell away from them Shegoggs, especially that John Jr. because that boy is not all there in the head," Sonny says.

Mary asks, "DeEtta, how is Julia doing? I hear that she is in a bad way after finding that boy's body hanging there like that. It must have been horrible for her to have been walking out there alone and walk up on something like that. You tell her that we are praying for her. And if she needs anything, just let us know," Mary adds.

"I'll let her know, Mama," DeEtta replies.

The next morning as everybody gets ready for church, there is a knock at the door. Sonny answers it. As he opens the door, there are two white men wearing suits standing on the other side.

"Can I help you, gentlemen?" Sonny asks.

They both then pull out badges, and one of them says, "We are with the Mississippi State Department of Revenue. And we are here investigating a report that someone in this area is operating an illegal whiskey still."

Sonny rubs his whiskers as he thinks about what the man has just said. He then replies, "I don't know nothing about no whiskey still being around here. We are all hardworking people."

Mary hears part of the conversation as she walks into the front room. She then walks over to the door and looks out to see who it is that Sonny is talking to.

"Well, if you see anything strange or something unusual, here is our card. Get in contact with us right away," one of the men says.

Mary then interrupts as the two gentlemen start to walk away, saying, "I know something that is both strange and unusual."

The two men stop, turn, and come back onto the porch. "You know something, ma'am?" the one agent asks.

"Yes! A young Black boy was lynched and burned less than five miles from here. And the local sheriff won't lift a finger to find out who done it!" Mary says.

Both agents' complexions turn pale as they struggle with how to respond to what Mary had just told them. "That's really not our department, ma'am," says the agent who has been doing most of the talking as they make their way to their car. They then drive off without even looking back.

"I guess they won't be coming back around here asking anymore questions for a while," Sonny says as he closes the door and he and Mary go and finish getting dressed for church.

As the church services begin, the whole congregation sits quietly prior to Rev. Mitchel starting his sermon. "Having sufferance and compassion for your fellow man, even though he refuses to do the same with regards to you, is what a Christian should do," the reverend says as he starts to speak. It is followed by several amens from the congregation. He then continues, "But being a Christian is sometimes like being a doctor because practicing medicine is what a doctor does. And a true Christian does the same with Christianity. He practices it.

"And for one to need to practice something means that he or she is not all the way there. They lack at least some of the required skills to have fully mastered it. For after one has mastered something, then there is little or no need for farther practice. And I say to you today, my dear congregation, I am practicing Christianity.

"And this I know because yesterday when we met with Sheriff Pickens and his deputies to request a shred of justice for the family of Willie Lee, it fell on deaf ears. And instead of getting justice, we got threatened! We got laughed at! And we got called names! And God is my witness today! Had I had a pistol in my hand, I would have shot him dead where he stood! So please! You all pray for me." The entire church stands to its feet and claps and shouts praise.

After the services are over, Rev. Mitchel comes over and thanks Sonny for what he had done yesterday. "You know, the devil is always at work. And for a brief time yesterday when I was talking to Sheriff Pickens, I completely forgot that I had a large part of my senior congregation standing there with me. And I want to thank you for pulling me back and allowing me to think about where I was and who was there with me," the reverend says as he shakes Sonny's hand.

As they leave the church, Marcus and DeEtta ride home together in his car. And Sonny, Sandy Earl, and Mary ride back in the truck. While driving down the road with Sonny leading the way, a police car pulls out from behind some bushes near the side of the road and pulls up behind Marcus's car. After tailing him for a moment or so, they turn on their flashing red lights.

As Marcus pulls over to the side of the road, the sheriff's car follows. Sonny sees what is happening, so he pulls over as well. After seeing Sonny pull over, the sheriff's car turns off its flashing lights and pulls off. As the car passes, Sonny sees that it is one of the same deputies who was looking out of the window laughing while Rev. Mitchel was talking with the sheriff.

After making it home, Sonny says to DeEtta and Sandy Earl, "That is why I don't want you all going places by yourselves."

Mary and DeEtta go inside to start putting dinner on the table as Sonny, Sandy Earl, and Marcus sit out on the porch. Sonny wants to ask Marcus about his father's strange habit of hiding in the woods and watching people but can't figure out how to word it so that it wouldn't offend him. So he doesn't bother to bring it up.

"Marcus, how are your parents doing these days?" Sonny asks.

"They are doing about as well as can be expected. Pops is either working in the fields or doing odd jobs that sometimes keep him working late into the night. Mama has a touch of the flu that she has been trying to shake for about a week now. But other than that, they are doing okay, I guess," Marcus answers.

After Mary and DeEtta get done setting the table, everyone goes inside and sits down and eats.

"That sure was a mighty fine dinner, Mrs. Wells," Marcus says as he gets ready to head home.

"You be sure and tell Bo and Nancy we said hello," Mary says as he walks out of the door.

The next morning, Sonny gets up earlier than usual. After hearing his father stirring around, Sandy Earl gets out of his bed and starts to get dress. Sonny stops him and tells him that he can sleep in.

After Sandy Earl gets back into bed, Sonny gets in his truck and drives out to the field where they had seen Bo hiding in the brush. Once there, he unlocks the shed and parks his truck inside next to the tractor.

Sonny then walks over to where he saw Bo go into the woods with the large sack and start to looks around. While looking around, he notices some weeds bent over from being stepped on. As he follows the trail of crushed plants into the woods, the birds suddenly stop their chirping, and a rather large red fox squirrel tries to hide itself by running around to the backside of the trunk of the tree that it was about to climb prior to having to acknowledge Sonny's presence.

As Sonny continues to venture deeper into the woods, the pre-sunrise morning light is soon blocked by the leaves on the trees. And he finds himself surrounded by a shadowy darkness. Not being able to follow the trail any farther, he finds a tree stump behind some brush and sits down on it and waits.

After a while, the large red fox squirrel forgets all about Sonny sitting only a few yards away. And it begins to search for fallen acorns once again. The birds also forget as they restart their ritual of chirping and scratching around in the fallen leaves for worms and other delicacies that might be hiding within. Not long after getting settled in, Sonny hears the distant sounds of roosters crowing as they christen the new day's sunrise. And shortly after the call from the roosters, the warm rays from the sun starts to gradually creep through the trees and make their way to the ground below.

Sonny leans back against the tree as he tries to make himself as comfortable as possible while waiting for Bo to return to his ostensibly special place. But like a well-taught thief in the night, aided by a soft breeze and the sound of the birds singing their rhythmic symphony of songs to praise the coming of a new day, sleep creeps upon him.

After sleeping for only a short while, Sonny is suddenly awakened by the sound of the bird's scurrying away and the red fox squirrel leaping onto the trunk of the tree a few feet away from where he is sitting. As the squirrel hides from the new intruder, he positions himself directly in front of Sonny as he moves around the tree's trunk to keep from being seen.

At first, Sonny can hardly hear the footsteps. But after a while, not only does he hear footsteps but the person can easily be seen. He walks as if he not only knows where he is going but is also on a mission to get there.

Sonny can tell right off that it's Bo. So he just sits and watches to see what it is that he is doing. Bo continues to walk for about another thirty yards after passing Sonny before stopping. He then moves several large tree branches. As he moves the last branch, Sonny can see why Bo didn't want anyone to know what he was doing because Bo had built himself a whiskey still.

"Hi, what are you doing there, Bo?" Sonny says as he gets up and starts to walk over toward him.

"Damn it, Sonny! I was doing fine until you damn near give me a heart attack. What are you doing back here?" Bo asks.

"Checking on my friend. I saw you standing in the tree line next to my field the other day and was wondering what was going on with you," Sonny answers. "Don't worry, your secret is safe with me," he adds.

The two friends then sit down and talk and reminisce about the days of old as they share a jug of Bo's corn whiskey.

CHAPTER 14

One Christmas

Summer 1990—The telephone rings and Jazmin answers it. "Mama, Dee! The telephone is for you. It's somebody named Amy Jean," Jazmin says as she yells down from upstairs.

Mama Dee gets up from the couch, makes her way over to the phone, picks it up, and says, "Hello! Hello!" But no is there. She then hangs up the phone and goes and sits back down on the couch.

About twenty minutes later, Jazmin comes downstairs to the family room and sits down next to Mama Dee and starts flipping through the channels on the TV.

"Who was that on the phone?" Mama Dee asks.

Jazmin replies, "Some lady named Amy Jean? At least, I think that what she said her name was. She said something about growing up with you."

After giving it some thought, Mama Dee asks, "Could she have said that her name was Irma Jean?"

Jazmin answers, "She could have. There was a lot of noise in the background, like she was on the highway or something."

Mama Dee tells Jazmin to go and get the phone and pull up the caller ID. The phone shows the number as "caller unknown."

As Jazmin watches the television, she notices that Mama Dee seems a little preoccupied with the phone. "You want me to put it back on the charger?" Jazmin asks.

"No, I'll hang on to it for a little bit in case she calls back," Mama Dee says as she looks down at the phone once more.

After a while, Stefan and Clarice come downstairs.

"Mama Dee, are you about ready to go to your doctor's appointment?" Clarice asks.

"Yes, I suppose so," Mama Dee replies as she gets up and picks up her purse.

Jazmin walks out onto the porch with them and sits down in the porch swing as she waves goodbye. Mama Dee, Stefan, and Clarice get in the car and drive off. Just as the car pulls out, the phone rings again. But this time, there is no one there to answer it.

Later that evening, after Mama Dee has returned from her doctor's appointment, the whole family sits down to eat dinner.

"So, how did your doctor appointment go, Mama Dee?" Jazmin asks.

Mama Dee replies, "The same as always. More tests, more pills. Did the person who called me earlier ever call back?"

"No, not that I know of," Jazmin replies.

"Oh yeah, that reminds me. Someone named Irma Jean called the other day for you, Mama Dee," Jamil says while stuffing his face with a piece of chicken. "She said that she was at your old house in Detroit, and your old neighbor, Ms. Davis, told her you had moved and gave her our phone number. She called the day that we were planting the flowers. Sorry, I forgot to tell you," Jamil says.

"Mama Dee, who is Irma Jean?" Jazmin asks.

Mama Dee then tells the story of who Irma Jean is and how they became friends.

* * *

Winter 1940—"Y'all hurry up and close that door!" Sonny shouts as Sandy Earl and Marcus bring in some more wood for the fire. "Don't look like this snow is ever going to stop. I can't remember the last time that we got anything more than a light dusting down here. Now, I'd bet you we got more than six inches out there," Sonny says after throwing another log on the fire.

After laying the last logs that he has in his arms onto the stack of wood next to the fireplace, Marcus says his goodbyes and leaves for work.

"That Marcus sure is a good young man. And, DeEtta, you are darn lucky to have him," Mary says as she turns her backside toward the fireplace to warm it.

"I know, Mama," DeEtta replies.

"And he's damn lucky to have my daughter too," Sonny adds as he nods his head, smiles, and winks at DeEtta.

Before long, the snow subsides, but the wind just keeps right on howling. It is as if it's trying to call someone back from the dead. Although Sonny and Mary live in one of the newer houses on the Shegogg place, it is as poorly insulated as are the older homes. But Sonny and Mary feel blessed because they were able to put away some of the money from the crops that year. So Sonny and Sandy Earl were able to do some insulating, and Mary was able to buy the material to make new quilts and blanket before the winter hit.

"Sandy Earl! It looks like the snowing has stopped. I need you and DeEtta to wrap up warm and take them stacks of old quilts over there up the hill and pass them out to whoever needs them. Make sure you go by the Johnsons and Higgins' place first because they got them young babies, and they lost almost everything in the mudslide. And don't tarry!" Mary says to them.

She then goes back in the bedroom and digs out four dollars and gives them to DeEtta with instructions to give each of the two families two dollars each. After DeEtta and Sandy Earl leave, Sonny pulls up two chairs next to the fire and asks Mary to come and sit with him.

"How much money do we have left in the sock?" Sonny asks.

Mary replies, "After paying for the funerals, putting something down on the truck, and buying a few things to get us through the winter, we have exactly one hundred ninety-two dollars."

Sonny sighs and says, "We are farther away from getting a place of our own than we were at the beginning of the planting season. I'm sorry, Mary."

"Sorry about what?" Mary asks.

"Sorry that I haven't been able to provide a better life for you and the children," Sonny says as he stirs into the fire.

Mary gently places her warm hand on top of his as it rests on the chair's arm. She then softly rubs her soft hand across his worn and callused skin and says, "Sonny, you are our life. And without you, I would have been lost. You are the most caring and hardworking man I have ever met. And no matter how hard or bad things get, you always put us first. And as long as you are in it, our lives couldn't be any better." She then lifts his overworked hand and kisses it.

As DeEtta knocks on the door of the Johnson's shack, at first, it seems as if no one is home because she doesn't hear anyone moving around inside. But as she starts to walk away, a child comes to the door. As the door opens, a little girl wrapped in a soiled, worn-out blanket sticks her head out.

"Is your mama home?" DeEtta asks.

The little girl says, "Yes" and opens the door wider. The house is dark, and the fire in the fireplace has long since burned itself out. DeEtta walks into the house as she follows the little girl into the back room.

After entering the back room, DeEtta sees both of the child's parents lying in bed. They are balled up together, shivering with fevers. And from the look and smell of things, they have been there for days.

"Run, get Mama!" DeEtta shouts to Sandy Earl as she takes off her coat and wraps the little girl in it. After seeing what was going on inside, Sandy Earl takes off running as fast as he can back to the house. Before long, Mary and Sonny are pulling up out front in the truck.

Mary barks out, "Sandy Earl! Go build a fire in the fireplace. DeEtta! Take that baby back to our house and get her warm and something to eat." She starts piling blankets on top of Mr. and Mrs. Johnson's shivering bodies.

Sonny quickly takes DeEtta and the little girl back to their house and returns with firewood for the fire. Sonny and Mary stay with the Johnsons until the early hours of the next morning. Sandy Earl continuously runs back and forth between the two houses for food, medicine, rags, etc. He makes so many trips back and forth that night that before long, he doesn't know if he is going or coming.

Once Mary is able to get the fevers to break, she makes them a big pot of stew to get them through the next day or so. She and Sonny then return home. When they get there, they find Sandy Earl and DeEtta awake. DeEtta had given the little girl a bath and put her down to sleep on a pallet in the front room next to the fire.

"How are they doing, Mama?" DeEtta asks.

"They are doing better. Your dad and I are going to get some sleep and go back to check on them later today," Mary answers as they head into their bedroom.

While Sonny and Mary are sleeping, DeEtta sits awake in the chair next to the fire, watching over the little girl as she sleeps. The child is sleeping so soundly it is as if she hasn't been this warm and comfortable for a long time. *Christmas is only a few weeks away, and my neighbors and their children are literally freezing to death. What kind of world is it that allows that?* DeEtta thinks to herself while looking at the little girl.

After the sun starts to make its way over the horizon, DeEtta gets up out of the chair and starts to make breakfast for everyone. Soon, the house is filled with the aroma of thick-sliced bacon frying in the pan. After a while, the rest of the family starts to stir.

"Good morning," Sandy Earl says as he walks out from one of the back rooms, stretching and yawning. Not long after, the little girl wakes up.

And while still lying with her head down on the pallet, she asks, "How is my mama and poppa doing?"

"They are doing just fine," DeEtta replies. DeEtta then fixes her a plate of food and calls her over to the table to eat. While the child is eating, Mary and Sonny gets out of bed and walks into the kitchen.

"I know I've seen you out playing before, but for the life of me, I can't remember your name! So what's your name?" Mary asks the little girl while fixing Sonny's plate.

The child can't answer right off because her mouth is full of food. Her jaws are so stuffed it is as if she hadn't had a decent bite to eat all winter. After swallowing the food and washing it down with several large gulps of milk, she replies, "Irma Jean."

"How old are you, Irma Jean?" Mary asks.

"I'll be eight on my birthday," Irma Jean replies before stuffing the last bit of a biscuit in her mouth.

After breakfast, Sonny and Mary get dressed and head out to check on Irma Jean's parents. While they are gone, Marcus stops by.

"Who is your newfound friend?" he asks as he walks into the house and sits down in one of the chairs by the fireplace.

"This is Irma Jean. She lives up on the hill not too far from where you all live," DeEtta answers.

"I thought she looked familiar," Marcus says.

Sandy Earl grabs the last of the biscuits and eggs and makes himself a sandwich before leaving to split firewood at the sawmill to make some extra money. "I'll see you guys around dinner time," he says as he walks out the door.

"So, how long have you two been friends?" Marcus asks while looking into the empty skillet and pan for a sample of the breakfast that he has missed.

"Since last night. And if you are hungry, I can fix you something to eat," DeEtta says.

Irma Jean walks over and sits down at the table next to DeEtta and lays her head against DeEtta's shoulder.

"This friendship must be a lot more serious than I thought. And if I didn't know any better, I'd think that she was trying to replace me," Marcus jokes.

"We'll talk about it at another time," DeEtta says while giving Marcus a solemn look to let him know that his jokes are inappropriate.

"Okay…" Marcus replies as he walks over to the window and looks out as if he was looking for someone to come and rescue him from the awkward moment. "I think that I might head on over to the sawmill with Sandy Earl and see if I can make some extra cash. We can probably use it for the wedding," Marcus says as he puts his coat back on. He then kisses DeEtta before leaving.

"So what do you want to do today?" DeEtta asks Irma Jean.

"I don't know. What is there to do?" Irma Jean asks.

"How about reading a good book?" DeEtta asks.

"I don't know how to read," Irma Jean replies as she looks down at the floor.

"Well…you know what? This is as good a time as any to learn," DeEtta says as she puts her hand under Irma Jean's chin and lifts her face up from looking at the floor. DeEtta takes Irma Jean over to where she keeps her books and asks her to pick out one.

After looking at several pictures on the cover, she chooses *Incidents in the Life of a Slave Girl* by Harriet Jacobs. "That is a great book, and it was written by someone who looks just like us," DeEtta says. They both then sit down in front of the fireplace. And DeEtta begins to teach Irma Jean how to read.

A few days later, Irma Jean's parents' health improves enough for her to return home. As DeEtta walks her home, she can tell that Irma Jean is sad.

"What's wrong?" DeEtta asks.

"I guess now that Mama and Poppa are not sick anymore, I won't be seeing you. Will I?" Irma Jean asks.

"Now, why in the world would you say that? I promised to teach you how to read. Didn't I?" DeEtta replies.

Irma Jean says, "Yes, you did say that" as she begins to smile.

"Well, that is just what I intend to do," DeEtta says. And as they continue to walk, they talk about things like the book that they had read, boys, and Irma Jean coming to the house two times a week for reading lessons with her new best friend.

Before long, it is Christmas Eve. And the whole house is bursting with the aromas of sweet potato pie, apple pie, stuffed turkey, and ham. The flavorful odors can even be smelt while standing in the front yard. As the family sits in the front room near the fire, Sonny drags a burlap sack from the back room. "So what is it that you want for Christmas?" Sonny asks Sandy Earl.

"A new pair of work boots would be nice," Sandy Earl answers. Sonny then reaches into the bag and pulls out a new pair of work boots and hands them to Sandy Earl.

Sandy Earl asks with a shocked look on his face, "How did you know that I wanted boots?"

Sonny replies, "To be perfectly honest with you, I didn't. But I did get tired of seeing you put cardboard over the holes in the soles of the ones that you are wearing."

After everyone finished laughing, Sonny then asks Mary the same question. After giving it some thought, Mary says, "A new pair of work boots!"

Everyone breaks out into laughter once more. Sonny then tells Sandy Earl to give him a hand. They both go out to the truck, and bring back a slightly used sewing machine that Sonny bought from Mrs. Loo.

Mary is so happy that she can't say a word. She just bursts out into tears. She then runs over to Sonny and hugs and kisses him as if they were the only two in the room. Sonny then asks DeEtta the same question. And without hesitation, DeEtta says, "Invite the Johnsons and the Higgins to spend Christmas with us."

ırlap sack on the floor. He and Mary a and Sandy Earl, and they hug in

Christmas evening in 1940, in the G2 house on the Snegogg's place, the Wells, the Higgins, and the Johnsons all sit together and have one of the best Christmas dinners that they have ever had. The air in the house might have been blessed with the aroma of pie and turkey with trimmings. But the hearts are filled with love and compassion.

CHAPTER 15
A Bittersweet January

Summer 1990—As the truck carrying the items from Mama Dee's old house pulls up the driveway, Stefan yells out to Jazmin and Jamil, "Hey guys, the truck is here. Get down here so that you can help unload it."

"I thought that was what we paid the movers to do," Jamil mumbles as he walks by.

"I heard that! And *we* are not paying anybody. Your mother and I are doing the paying, and you need to shut your mouth and do what you are told to do, mister!" Stefan says while opening the door to the detached garage that they had a contractor build prior to them moving in.

As the truck is being unloaded, Mama Dee is directing everyone on where to put her things in the garage.

"Jamil, take them two boxes that you are carrying up to my room and sit them next to my dresser. I need to go through them and take out some things before storing them here in the garage. And be careful with them!" Mama Dee says as she tries to take one of the boxes from one of the guys that are unloading the truck.

"Mama! What are you doing?" Stefan asks as he intercepts the box. "Now, you promised not to get in the way. So go back over there, sit down, and just direct. Please, Mama!" Stefan says while standing motionlessly between her and the guy who's unloading the truck, waiting for her to comply. As Mama Dee makes her way back over to her perch, she mumbles words of discontent.

After they are done unloading the truck, Mama Dee gets on the elevator and heads up to her room. Once inside of her room, she drags one of the boxes that Jamil brought up over next to her rocking chair by the window. And as she is about to start going through the items in the box, Clarice knocks on the door.

"Come on in, it's not locked," Mama Dee says.

"I brought you a glass of water. It's time to take your medicine," Clarice says as she hands the glass to Mama Dee. Mama Dee thanks her before taking her pills and washing them down with the water that she brought her.

"What's in the boxes?" Clarice asks.

"Just some old pictures and things," Mama Dee replies.

"Okay if I look at some of them with you?" Clarice asks.

"Sure!" Mama Dee replies.

As Clarice pulls the first stack of pictures from one of the boxes, an envelope falls to the floor. Clarice picks up the envelope and hands it to Mama Dee. Mama Dee hesitates for a moment before taking it.

"What's the matter? Clarice asks.

"Oh…nothing," Mama Dee replies as she takes the envelope and opens it. "It's just…I didn't even know that I still had this."

"What is it?" Clarice asks.

"It's a telegram to my mother," Mama Dee explains.

"Must have been an important message to send as a telegram, huh?" Clarice asks.

"Yes, it was. Especially back then," Mama Dee says as she starts to tell Clarice the story about her mother getting it.

* * *

January 1941—As a cold wind blows across the open field, Sonny, Sandy Earl, and Jimmy toss the last few bales of hay onto the back of the truck.

"Thanks for giving us a hand with this, Jimmy. You were a big help," Sonny says as they all three climb into the cab of the truck. As they are getting ready to drive off, they see Marcus's car coming across the field in their direction. And he is flying!

Marcus slams on the brakes as he pulls up next to the truck. DeEtta is sitting in the car with him, and she is crying. "Jimmy! You need to get to the hospital as fast as you can. It's your father! He got hurt over at the sawmill. Jump in. I'll take you!" Marcus says.

Jimmy quickly hops out of the truck and gets into the car with Marcus and DeEtta. The airborne dust from the field can be seen from far away as it hovers high into the air as the car speeds off into the distance.

"I sure hope that Mr. Nathan will be all right," Sandy Earl says to his father as they drive off. After dropping the bales of hay off at the pasture where Sonny keeps his two milking cows and the old mules that he once plowed the fields with. They head home to tell Mary about what has happened to Nathan.

As they pull up to the house, they can tell that someone had already stopped by and told her because Mary is sitting on the front porch as if she is waiting for them to get home.

"Where is Jimmy?" Mary asks.

"He is on his way to the hospital. Marcus and DeEtta came by the field and got him," Sonny answers.

"Lord, have mercy! That boy already done lost his mother. And now this!" Mary says as she walks back into the house.

Sonny and Sandy Earl walk in behind her.

"I think we need to go to the hospital and be with him," Mary says as she puts Sonny and Sandy Earl's dinner on the table.

"We can do that as soon as we get done eating. And if you would, please fix Jimmy a plate of food so that we can take with us. I don't think that he has had a bite to eat since breakfast this morning," Sonny says as he and Sandy Earl sit down and starts to eat.

After eating, they head off to the hospital. Once they arrive at the hospital, they find out that Nathan has been taken seventy miles away to a hospital in Memphis to have emergency surgery and that Marcus, DeEtta, and Jimmy are on their way there.

"I guess we might as well head on back home. I'm sure DeEtta will let us know if there is anything that we need to do," Sonny says.

As they walk back to the truck, they see Sara being dropped off at the hospital.

"Sara!" Mary calls out as she waves her hand in the air to get her attention. Sara sees them and comes over. "They have taken Nathan to a hospital in Memphis to get operated on," Mary tells her.

"Jimmy is on his way there along with Marcus and DeEtta; they are taking him. They were gone when we got here," Sonny adds.

Just then, Marcus's car pulls up. "They told us that you guys were on your way to Memphis," Sonny says.

"We were. Then Jimmy thought that Sara would want to be there too. So we stopped by her house to get her, and her little sister told us that she was on her way here," DeEtta says as Sara is getting into the car. As they drive off, Mary tells them to be careful and that they all will be praying for Nathan.

Once Mary and Sonny are back home, Mary makes a pot of coffee, and she and Sonny sit in front of the fireplace. While sipping on their cups of coffee and staring at the flames, Mary reflects on just how fragile life can be.

She thinks back on when the Klan had attacked Sonny. It ended horribly. What if they had killed him? And where would she and their children be today if that had happened?

Sonny's thoughts are more focused on DeEtta, Marcus, and Sara because he knows all too well that whenever a Black man traveled the Delta's roads at night, he was putting his life on the line. And the most dangerous hazards would more likely be human in nature, rather than mechanical or animal. The race haters and the Klan members are always looking for an opportunity to make a statement.

As the night passes and the morning makes its presence known, Mary and Sonny are awakened by the sounds of Sandy Earl getting ready for work.

"Did you guys sleep there all night?" Sandy Earl asks. Neither Sonny nor Mary reply as they both stretch and yawn. "I'm headed uptown to help unload some trucks over at the Shegogg's store. They have their supply trucks coming in this morning, and Steven told me that he would pay me to unload them. You guys try and get some rest now, and I'll see you when I get back," Sandy Earl says before walking out the door.

After collecting her thoughts, Mary gets cleaned up and starts to make breakfast while Sonny goes to milk and feed the cows. As he drives up to pasture where the animals are kept, he sees Bo coming out of the woods.

"What are you doing out here at this time of the morning? Don't tell me that you moved that whiskey still *again*?" Sonny asks.

"Okay, I won't tell you that I moved the still again," Bo replies as they both laugh.

"Did you hear about what happened to Nathan?" Bo asks.

"Yes, I did hear that he got hurt. But I didn't hear how," Sonny replies.

"Well…what I heard was that he was working with the big chop saw at the mill when the bracing stake that holds back the stack of debarked logs gave way. And the whole stack of logs came rolling down on top of him. One of the guys that were there said that he wasn't breathing when they took him away."

Sonny shakes his head as Bo offers him a shot of the previous night's batch of moonshine, which he gladly accepts along with several others. After making it back to the house, Sonny staggers through the door and sits down at the table. He sees that Mary has covered his now cold breakfast with a cloth in an attempt to keep it warm before going into the bedroom, lying down, and falling off to sleep.

After eating his cold breakfast, Sonny goes into the bedroom and lies down next to Mary. They both sleep for several hours, giving Sonny an opportunity to sober up around the same time that Mary wakes up.

"I need to go to town and pick up a few things from the Chinamen," Mary says. Sonny, still filling some of the effects of the moonshine, gets up and gets dressed.

While driving down the road, Sonny asks, "What are you going to the Chinamen for?"

"With all that's going on, I just need to get out of the house. So I thought that I might as well start looking at some material to make the dresses that I'm going to wear at DeEtta and Sara's weddings," Mary answers.

Sonny doesn't say anything in reply to her reason why; he just grunts and continues to drive. As they pull up in front of the store, they are greeted by Mrs. Loo in her typical high energy fashion. "Good afternoon Mary!" Mrs. Loo says as she walks over and gives her a hug. "How is the sewing machine working out for you? I hope you liked it. We were happy to know that Sonny was buying it for you," Mrs. Loo says.

"It's working great! That is part of the reason why we are here. I need to look at some material to make my dress for DeEtta's wedding," Mary replies. "How is Mr. Loo doing?" Mary asks as she and Mrs. Loo walk over to where the different types of material that Mary might be interested in are kept.

"I'm going over to the post office to see if the seeds I ordered have come in yet," Sonny says before walking back out the shop door. While walking over to the post office, Sonny sees John Jr. and several of his friends sitting in his car drinking. Sonny manages to keep from making eye contact with them as he passes until he hears someone in the group say, "Hey nigger! Aren't you the nigger that my daddy and his boys turned into one of them there eunuchs a while back?"

They all then burst out into laughter. Although the words shouted at him cut through his soul like a hot knife cuts through butter, Sonny just looks down toward the ground and continues to walk past. While looking through the window of the store, Steven can see that John Jr. and his friends are trying to stir up trouble. So he walks outside and goes over to the car and asks them to leave.

John Jr. hops out the car and walks up to Steven as if he was going to hit him. But Steven doesn't move an inch. Instead, he looks at his brother as if he could kill him and not even attend the funeral. Seeing that John Jr.'s attempt to intimidate his brother wasn't working, some of his friends hop out of the car, grab him by the arms, and pull him back into the car. John Jr. then starts his car and angrily burns rubber down through the center of town. Someone in the car yells out another ethnic obscenity at Sonny as the car passes him.

After entering the post office, Sonny checks their post office box for the seeds. Seeing that it is empty, he starts to leave. As he leaves, the mail clerk yells out to him, "Is Mary Wells some kin to you?"

"Yes, she is my wife," Sonny replies.

"You just missed the Western Union delivery guy. He was here asking for her address. I sent him out to your place," the mail clerk says. Sonny heads back over to the Chinamen store to tell Mary about the telegram.

After Sonny tells Mary that she has some kind of delivery waiting for her at the house, she hurries up and finishes up her business with Mrs. Loo, and they head for home. While driving along, Mary and Sonny both wonder who in the world would be sending her a telegram. Mary has never gotten a telegram before. The only time that she even had gotten a letter was because she had ordered something through the mail, which rarely happened.

After thinking about it for a spell, Mary starts to wonder, *Maybe it's bad news?* After all, she hasn't heard from any of her relatives in over thirty years. *Maybe something has happened to one of them*, she starts to think as her feelings of excitement start to teeter toward a feeling of concern. As they pull up to the house, they see that Marcus and DeEtta have made it back from Memphis and are standing on the porch. DeEtta has the letter in her hand.

Mary and Sonny hop out of the car, and DeEtta runs over to them and says, "Look, Mama, you have a telegram."

Mary takes the envelope from DeEtta and opens it. While she is reading it, she almost falls to the ground as her knees buckle and tears start to flow from her eyes.

Sonny catches her. And as he puts his arm around her, he asks, "Who is it from? And what is wrong?"

Mary replies, "There isn't anything wrong! Everything is right! It's from my sister Betty! And she, her husband Ed, their three kids, and seven grandkids are living in California. And doing well," Mary says as she sits down on the steps of the porch.

After talking to DeEtta, they find out that Nathan is going to pull through also. The whole family then rejoices as a long and bittersweet day comes to an end.

CHAPTER 16
Sara's Wedding

Summer 1990—As Clarice and Mama Dee continue to go through the boxes, they are joined by Jazmin and Jamil.

"Mama! Jazmin keeps changing the channel on the TV while I'm trying to watch the ballgame. Will you tell her to stop it?" Jamil says as they both burst into Mama Dee's room.

"I had the television first, and nobody wants to watch a stupid ballgame!" Jazmin replies.

"There are at least five other televisions in this house. Why in the world are you two fighting over that one?" Clarice asks. "I'll tell you what! Being that you two can't sit and watch television together—*or* apart—both of you come in here and sit down and look at me then!" Clarice shouts.

Stefan hears the commotion and comes into the room to see what is going on. After seeing his father, Jamil starts to plead his case to him. But after he sees the look on his mother's face, he quickly decides that it might not be a good idea.

Stefan looks over at Clarice and can see the frustration on her face as she stares at the children with an intimidating scowl on her face. Mama Dee looks up, but only momentarily, as it all plays out.

"What are you two up to?" Stefan asks Mama Dee and Clarice as he walks past Jazmin and Jamil, who are sitting at the foot of Mama Dee's bed and trying not to make eye contact with their mother.

"Just going through some of your mother's stuff," Clarice answers while still eyeballing Jazmin and Jamil.

"I think I'm going to take a ride to the store and take them two with me before they get into any more trouble. Do you guys need anything?" Stefan asks as he signals to Jazmin and Jamil to head toward the car.

"I'm fine. How about you, Mama Dee?" Clarice asks.

"I'm good," Mama Dee says as she pulls another stack of pictures from one of the boxes.

Soon after Stefan and the children drive off, Mama Dee looks at one of the pictures that she has pulled from the box and starts to laugh. She laughs so hard and so long that at first, Clarice is about to call Stefan back to the house. "What is it, Mama Dee?" Clarice asks as she starts to laugh at Mama Dee laughing. Mama Dee then stops laughing long enough to show Clarice the picture.

In the picture were a young Mama Dee and two of her friends. One of them is wearing a wedding dress. Clarice looks at the picture and doesn't see anything that looks funny.

"What are you laughing at, Mama Dee?" Clarice asks.

Mama Dee then tells her the story of when the photograph was taken.

* * *

Early Spring 1941—As the church services are winding down, Sara, DeEtta, and Julia sit next to one another in their usual seats behind Ms. Lillie and her friends.

Sara tells DeEtta and Julia, "The doctor came to Jimmy's house and told him some news about the injuries that his father received in his accident at the mill. And after the doctor had left the house, Jimmy was very upset. I ran over to him, and that's when he told me that his father only has a short time."

No sooner had the services ended and people are starting to walk to the cars and wagons. Sara starts to get words of sympathy.

"You tell Nathan and Jimmy that the whole church will be praying for them," Rev Mitchel says to Sara as she walks past him.

"How in the world did he find out about it when you just told us about it?" DeEtta asks Sara. And before Sara can answer, she sees the how in action.

Ms. Lillie and her friends are literally spreading the word so fast that one would think they were being paid to do so.

"I didn't know that Nathan had taken a turn for the worst. And I just saw him out back of his house chopping wood last week. Sara, you be sure and tell Jimmy that if he needs anything, don't hesitate to ask," Sonny says as he and Mary pass Sara while walking to their truck.

The next morning, Jimmy gets up early and goes to Sara's house and knocks on the door. Sara's father answers, and Jimmy can tell right off that he is recovering from another one of his nightly drinking binges.

"Good morning, sir," Jimmy says.

"Good morning. And for what reason are you knocking on my door this early on a Monday morning?" Sara's father replies.

"I'm here to ask if it would be okay for me and Sara to get married this coming Saturday instead of waiting until next month, sir," Jimmy says.

Sara steps out from behind the door. Jimmy, while staring into Sara's eyes, says, "Sir, I know that I don't have much to offer, but I am a hard worker, and I will do anything it takes to take care of her and make her happy."

Sara's father then says, "I heard about your father, and tell him that we are all pulling for him. I suppose it won't hurt anything by you all moving the date up. Hell! Neither one of us got much money to put toward a big wedding anyway." He and his wife then give their okay to move things up.

Jimmy then tells Sara, "I'll be back, I need to go and take care of something." Unbeknownst to Sara, Jimmy is going to see Big John.

Knowing that Big John didn't allow people of color to set foot on his front porch unless they were painting or cleaning it, Jimmy knocks on the back door. Ms. Lillie, who is their housekeeper, answers the door.

"Is Mr. Shegogg in?" Jimmy asks.

Before Ms. Lillie could answer or ask, "Why are you here to see him?" Big John pulls the door open wider. "What do you want, little Nathan?" Big John asks.

Jimmy answers, "Mr. Shegogg, I know you been good to my family, sir, and I thank you for that. But I want to get married to Sara, and we would like to get a place of our own. I promise to pay you back by cleaning up and planting that sixty acres of land down on the other side of the creek, sir. All we need is a truck to help clear it and some furniture to put in the house that we will be renting from you. And if you could see fit to give us a loan of about two hundred dollars, I can build on to the house so that my father can move in with us. I will pay you back ten dollars a month from the side jobs that I been working. I'll will pay you back every dime with interest, sir! I give you my word on that."

Big John looks at Jimmy and sees what he saw in his father many years ago, someone who would do what he is told, knows his place in life, and would work himself to death for you. After acting as if he is giving the proposal some thought, Big John replies, "I heard about your father not doing so well. I'm truly sorry to hear that. But before I agree to anything, there is the question that we need to deal with pertaining to your father's debt. Are you willing to take on that debt as well?" Big John asks.

Jimmy looks over at Ms. Lillie, who is acting as if she is cleaning, but he can tell that she is listening to every word. "Yes, sir," Jimmy replies.

"Okay, I'm going to give you a chance to make something of yourself, boy. Just remember one thing! *Don't try and fuck Big John!*"

"No, sir, no, sir, Mr. Shegogg. I would never do that! My daddy worked his whole life right here on your land.

And if the good Lord is willing, I'm going to do the same thing as my daddy did."

Big John then says, "Go uptown to Ford dealer and ask for Sam. I'll give him a call and let him know that you are coming. Then go over to the Chinaman and tell him I sent you. And you and your little bride go ahead and pick out a few things for your new home. Y'all can move into the S house. It's vacant right now."

Big John then tells Jimmy to wait as he goes into the den. He later returns with three hundred dollars in cash and hands it to Jimmy. "I'm giving you a little extra cash. I know it's hard starting out, and you can pay it all back like we agreed," Big John says as he hands Jimmy the money.

"Thank you, thank you, thank you, sir," Jimmy says as Big John turns and walks away.

After getting the truck, Jimmy and Sara are busy the next few days picking up furniture and moving things into their new home. As the week comes to an end, Sara stops by to see DeEtta.

"How are the wedding plans coming?" DeEtta asks.

"Actually, Jimmy and I decided to move up the date with Jimmy's father being in a bad way and all," Sara says.

"So... when is the new date?" DeEtta asks.

"This coming Saturday. We decided to do something small. But there is one thing that we need from you and Marcus," Sara says.

After getting over the initial shock, DeEtta says, "Sure! Whatever yawl need. You know, we are here for you!"

"We want you guys to be our maid of honor and best man," Sara says.

DeEtta hugs Sara as her eyes fill with tears. "We would be honored," DeEtta says. "Where are you guys planning on living?" DeEtta asks.

"Jimmy worked out something with Mr. Shegogg for us to rent one of his houses," Sara answers.

"I somehow envisioned us all moving out of Mississippi once we all got married," DeEtta says while wiping the tears from her eyes and sniffling.

"Yeah, me too," Sara replies. Sara then walks over and opens the door, and before leaving, she says, "You do know that I love you like a sister, don't you? And there is no time or distance that could ever change that."

DeEtta nods her head and says, "I love you to." Sara then leaves.

When Saturday arrives, they all meet up at Jimmy's house to get it ready for the wedding.

"Why don't you boys run down the hill to our house and get those boxes with the ribbons in them so that we can decorate the front porch a little?" DeEtta asks.

While the guys are gone, DeEtta, Julia, and Sara talk about their growing up together and how much things have changed since they have grown up. They also talk about how they hope things will be in the future and how they will be friends forever, no matter where life takes them.

After noticing that she and DeEtta are doing all of the talking, Julia asks Sara, "You seem kind of quiet. Is everything okay?"

"Sure! Everything is just fine. It's just a little bit of the wedding jitters," Sara answers.

"Cheer up, girl! It's your wedding day," Julia says as she gives her a hug. Once the guys return, DeEtta tells them to hang the ribbon out front while they work on moving some of the stuff from the front room into one of the back rooms.

After the ribbons were hung and the front room cleaned and decorated with flowers and hanging lace, Someone with a little bit of imagination could imagine themselves not being deep in the Delta in some little repressive part of Mississippi but somewhere where the air smells of freedom and the bondage of Jim Crow is nonexistent.

The tiny shack has been transformed into something that is best described in the words of Mary Wells as she steps into the small house prior to the start of the wedding: "This place is beautiful." As DeEtta and Julia step out onto the porch where Jimmy and Marcus are waiting all dressed up in their Sunday bests, the small crowd of about fifteen people releases a unanimous "Aww."

Then comes the time for the bride to walk out. With her father by her side, Sara steps onto the porch. She is immediately greeted by claps and praises for her beauty and the stunning wedding dress that Mrs. Loo has loaned her to wear. Rev. Mitchel then performs the ceremony.

Once the vows had been made and the broom leaped across, Sara tosses her bouquet into the air. After being fumbled by several other would-be brides, it lands in the arms of Julia. Julia smiles as she displays her bouquet of orchids and angel's breath among the crowd.

"Sara! Get over here so that we can take a picture," DeEtta says as she pulls Sara and Julia by the arms.

Mrs. Loo sets up her camera as DeEtta, Sara, and Julia pose. After the first flash, DeEtta says, "Mrs. Loo, can you take another one for me to keep? I want to remember this day forever." As the camera flash goes off once more, in the not so far distance, just beyond the tree line, Steven is captured in the photo as he sits and watches the festivities.

The early evening soon becomes the night as the well-wishers dance and sip on punch spiked with Bo's finest spirits. And while everyone is still mingling in and around the shack, Julia sneaks off into the woods to talk with Steven. "I've been watching you hiding over here all evening. What going on?" Julia asks as she walks up to Steven.

"Nothing really. I was just watching the wedding and the partying," Steven answers.

"When are you planning on getting married? I know all of those little white girls are just dying to get their hooks in you," Julia Ann asks as she sips on her cup of punch. "You want a sip of punch?" she asks.

"Sure!" Steven says as he takes the cup and drinks out of it. Julia and Steven talk well into the night. And as the conversation draws to an end, Steven watches over her from a distance as she walks home.

The next morning, Sara and Jimmy spend the entire day inside their new house hanging curtains and working on things. The following day, they move Nathan in with them, and Jimmy makes some rails for his newly acquired pickup truck so that he can stack more stuff on the back of it.

"What are you working on?" Marcus asks after stopping by for a visit. Jimmy closes the front door behind him as he walks out onto the front porch.

"Just adding some rails to my truck's sides so that I can carry a larger load. I need you to do me another favor," Jimmy asks Marcus.

"What is it?" Marcus asks.

"I'm going to be working that piece of land down by the creek, getting it ready for planting next season, and I don't have a lot of time. So, me, Sara, and Daddy are going to camp out down there until I can get a handle on it," Jimmy says. "All I need is for you to stop by the house every now and then and light a lamp or move things around on the porch so that people will think that we are here. That way, nobody will come in and take our things while we are away," Jimmy says.

"Sure! I can do that. And after you figure out what you need to do on the land, let me know. I'll spend a few weekends down there, giving you a hand," Marcus says.

As the weeks pass and the temperature starts to warm, DeEtta and Marcus's wedding day draws nearer, and DeEtta starts to miss Sara. After talking to Marcus and convincing him to take a drive down to see them, she realizes that she wasn't sure exactly where about on the creek they were located at. So, after driving around for hours, they decided to go by the house.

Marcus pulls the key that Jimmy had given him from his pocket and opens the door. And when DeEtta walks in, she is speechless. Marcus sees the look on her face and asks, "What's wrong, honey?"

"I thought you said that they asked you to keep an eye on their house for them," DeEtta says.

"They did! And I have been!" Marcus replies.

"Well, if you've been watching the house for them. How could someone have come in here and stolen all of their new furnishings that they bought? And leave all of this junk behind?" DeEtta asks.

"I never bothered to go in. I just check the doors and walked around the house," Marcus answers.

And at that moment, Marcus and DeEtta realizes what has happened, and they both start to laugh. They laugh so hard that they literally fall down on the floor.

It wasn't until two days later that Big John figures out what has happened. And by then, they have been gone for almost a month. Big John raises all kinds of hell, but Jimmy, Sara, the three hundred dollars, the truck loaded with new furniture, and Nathan, whom he had cheated for years, were nowhere to be found.

CHAPTER 17

Poppa

Summer 1990—"Mama Dee, you need to stay in bed like the doctor told you to. Or at least until you get stronger," Clarice says after walking into Mama Dee's room and catching her trying to make her bed. "And besides, we are paying that nurse good money to take care of you after your treatments. So please, get back in bed," Clarice adds.

Stefan then comes into the room. "Mama! What are you doing?" he asks.

"I'm trying to make my own damn bed if you two would leave me alone," Mama Dee says as she continues to fix the bed.

"Come on, Clarice let's leave her alone. If she insists on doing things that she knows that she shouldn't be doing, it's on her. But I'll tell you one thing! When you fall flat on your butt and break something, they are going to confine you to a wheelchair! And if you think that you don't like lying in that bed while you recuperate from your treatments, you most certainly won't like being in that wheelchair all of the time," Stefan says before storming out of the room.

Mama Dee stops what she is doing and walks over to her rocking chair next to the balcony doors and sits down and starts to look out of the window. "This damn chemotherapy. I don't know which is worst, these treatments or the not being able to do much after having them," Mama Dee says to Clarice.

"I know it's hard for you, but all Stefan is trying to do is take care of his mother, whom he loves very much!" Clarice replies.

Mama Dee responds, "I know. And I'm sorry for yelling at you and Stefan. But lying there in that bed makes me feel like I'm just lying around waiting to die. And that's not how I intend for you, Stefan, or my grandchildren to remember me. That is, if I have anything to say about it."

Clarice replies, "Now, Mama Dee, that is enough about death. Ain't nobody going anywhere anytime soon. So please! Let's change the subject."

Clarice then kisses Mama Dee on the forehead and leaves the room. While sitting there, Mama Dee reaches onto the dresser and picks up a picture of her Mama and Poppa. And while looking at the picture, she starts to recall a time from her past.

* * *

Early Spring 1941—"Poppa, why don't you just stay in bed this morning? I can go feed the animals and start turning the fields by myself, so get back in bed. I got this!" Sandy Earl says as he helps his father back into the bedroom.

"Thanks, Sandy Earl!" Mary says." Lord knows that that man needs to rest if he is ever going to get over this flu. The doctor done told him that he needs to rest! But he is so darn stubborn and won't listen to anybody!" Mary makes another pot of hot tea to mix Sonny's medicine in that the doctor gave him. That way, he can drink it down instead of taking pills, which is something he hates doing.

"I know, Mama. He has always had to work, so lying around is something that he isn't used to doing. Heck! He has been working in the fields ever since he was six years old. Work is all that he knows," Sandy Earls says to Mary before walking out the door.

Just as Sandy Earl is starting to drive off, DeEtta comes running out of the house and flags him down. "You almost forgot this," she says as she hands him the bag containing his lunch through the driver's side window.

"DeEtta! Help Mama with Poppa while I'm gone. Okay?" Sandy Earl asks. DeEtta nods her head as he then drives off.

While Sandy Earls is off working in the fields, there is a knock on the door. DeEtta answers it. After opening the door, she sees a young Black man wearing a suit standing on the porch.

"Yes, may I help you?" DeEtta asks while looking him up and down.

"Are you the lady of the house?" he asks.

"No, not really. She is busy at the moment. What do you want with her? I'm her daughter, so you can tell me, and I will tell her," DeEtta says.

The gentlemen then explains, "I sell the best knives in the world. And I would like to show you our 1941 special addition of fine cutlery." As he finishes his sale pitch, Mary walks up to the door. "Hi there, I take it that you are the lady of the house?" he asks as he extends his hand to Mary. Mary shakes his hand as he introduces himself. "My name is Marques Summers, and I work for the Southerland Cutlery company of Philadelphia. And I would like to introduce you to a line of cutlery that will last you for a lifetime," he says.

Mary attempts to tell him that she wasn't interested. But the word "no" only seems to make him try harder.

"I'll tell you what, Mary. It is okay if I call you Mary, isn't it?" he asks. Mary nods her head yes as he continues on with his sales pitch. "If you just buy one of my knives for a dollar, not only do I guarantee that you will love it, but I will sharpen it once a month for you for free. This is my new territory, and I will be through here every month to check on you. What do you say, Mary?" Marques says as he concludes his spiel.

Mary digs into her coin purse and hands him a dollar. The money was not only for the knife but also to end the conversation so that she could go back to the bedroom and tend to Sonny. After transacting the business, Marques picks up his suitcase of cutlery and makes his way to the next house on the row.

A couple of hours later, Julia stops by the house to check on DeEtta and see how Sonny is doing. "How is your father doing?" Julia asks after hearing him coughing.

"About the same as yesterday," DeEtta replies.

"If you all need me to do anything, just let me know," Julia says.

"Thanks, we will," DeEtta replies. "Did you happen to run into the knife salesman on your way down the hill?" DeEtta asks.

"Who—Marques?" Julia asks.

"Yes, I do believe that he did say that his name was Marques," DeEtta replies.

"Was this the first time that you saw him?" Julia asks.

"Well…yes," DeEtta answers.

"Marques has been coming around for months now trying to sell those knives of his. I'm shocked that he hasn't stopped by here before," Julia says as DeEtta walks over to the stove and puts another log inside of it before pouring Julia and herself a hot cup of water from the teapot to make them a cup of tea.

While sitting at the table and sipping on their cups of tea, Julia asks, "So! Do you think he's cute?"

"Who?" DeEtta asks.

"Girl! Don't play with me. You know who I'm talking about—Marques!" Julia says as they both start to giggle.

"I suppose so," DeEtta confesses.

After discussing Marques's finer attributes, DeEtta says, "I sometimes sit and wonder how Jimmy and Sara are doing. I sure hope that things are going well for them. I miss my girl so much!"

Julia shakes her head in agreement as they finish drinking their cups of tea. As Julia is getting ready to leave, Mary comes out of the bedroom and closes the door behind her.

"How are you doing this morning, sweetheart?" Mary asks Julia as she sets the dishes from Sonny's breakfast on the table.

"I'm doing just fine, Mrs. Wells," Julia replies.

"Tell your mama I said hi, okay?" Mary says to her as she walks out the door and onto the front porch.

Julia replies, "Yes, Ma'am, I will."

While Julia is walking up the road toward home, she sees someone running toward her as fast as he can. It is Marques. And he is running as if his life depended on him getting to where he is going as soon as he possibly can. As he runs past Julia, she attempts to speak to him. But he flies past her as if she isn't even there.

Julia can tell that he has been running for a while because he has lost his suit coat, the suitcase containing his fine cutlery utensils, and his shoes. His once nicely starched white shirt is no longer tucked neatly in his trousers, and he is sweating profusely.

Before Julia can get a second sentence out of her mouth, he makes a sharp turn and is now heading toward the row of houses where DeEtta lives. No sooner had he made the turn than Julia sees several white men on horses coming down the road.

It's John Jr. and some of his friends. As John Jr. and his friends come upon Julia, John Jr. asks her, "Did you see a nigger come running down this way wearing a suit?"

Julia looks down toward the ground and says, "No, sir, I didn't."

One of John Jr. friends then says, "That lying bitch. I know damn well she saw him. He must have run right past her." He starts to get down off his horse.

"That there is Steven's piece of ass. And if you fuck with her, he is probably going to kill you," John Jr. says while looking at his friend with a matter-of-fact look on his face.

After hearing that, his friend changes his mind about getting off the horse. And they all ride off to continue their search. As they are riding away, John Jr. says, "If you happen to see that nigger, you tell him that the next time he set foot on our front porch, we are going to find him and skin him like a grape. You have yourself a good day there now, Ms. Julia."

Meanwhile back at DeEtta's house, "Did you hear that, Mama?" DeEtta says. "Hear what?" Mary replies. "That thumping sound. It sounds like it coming from under the house." DeEtta says. DeEtta then goes outside to see what is making the noise.

As she opens the front door, she sees John Jr. and his friends on their horses riding past. She waits until they have ridden out of sight and then goes out around back and looks underneath the house. And to her surprise, she sees the neighbors bluetick hound dog, Rex, and Marques. Both of them are shivering as if they had eaten a peach pit and were trying to pass it.

"Get out from under there and come on in the house," DeEtta says while kneeling down. And as Marques is crawling out from underneath the house, Julia comes running down the road.

"Oh my God. I thought for sure that they were going to catch you," Julia says while trying to catch her breath.

As the three of them go into the house, DeEtta ask Marques, "What in the world did you do to get them so pissed off at you?"

"All I did was knock on the door. And before I knew it, this colored woman who looked like the maid started to scream something about, 'Get off this porch!' And then, an old white woman started screaming the same thing."

"So I left. A short while later, while I was sitting on the ground trying to get the rocks out of my shoes, those white men on them there horses started shooting at me. They would have caught me if I hadn't cut through some thorn bushes and run across that cemetery. A little while after that was when you saw me running down the road," Marques says.

"By the way, where are you staying?" Julia asks.

"Right now, I'm living in a tent down by the creek. That's only until I can make enough money to maybe rent a place," Marques says.

DeEtta then goes into the back room where Sandy Earl sleeps and gets his old work boots and brings them back out. She then gives them to Marques. "Here, you can have these. They have a hole in the bottom, but it beats going barefoot," she says as she hands him the boots. "If I was you, I would be looking for another place to camp out at," DeEtta says.

After hearing bits and pieces of the conversation from their bedroom, Mary shouts from the bedroom, "And the answer is no! He can't stay here!"

After hearing what Mary had said, Julia says, "I suppose you could come and stay with us for a couple of days. But I need to ask Poppa first."

So while Marques lay low at DeEtta's house, Julia goes home to ask her parents if it would be okay for Marques to stay with them for a while. Before long, Sandy Earl returns from the field. And as he walks into the house, he sees Marques sitting in the chair next to the fireplace wearing his old boots.

Sandy Earl looks over at Marques as he sits there looking all shuffled and sweaty. He then looks over at DeEtta. DeEtta starts to say something, but before she can speak, Sandy Earl smiles. Knowing that his sister has a heart as big as the moon itself, he doesn't give her the opportunity to explain. He just keeps smiling as he shakes his head and goes into his room.

Before long, Marcus is off work and is knocking at the door. As DeEtta opens the door, the first thing that Marcus notices is Marques sitting in the chair next to the fireplace. After hearing Marcus's voice, Mary and Sandy Earl come out of their rooms because, big heart or not, DeEtta has some explaining to do to Marcus. And Mary and Sandy Earl don't want to miss one word of it.

As DeEtta attempts to explain the chain of events that led to how a good-looking stranger with his clothes all shuffled and wearing her brother's old boots come to be sitting in their front room, Sandy Earl and Marcus listen attentively. Mary, who had witnessed part of what had happened firsthand, chuckles to herself as DeEtta searches for the right words.

Just when DeEtta was almost done explaining, Julia knocks at the door.

"Well...I asked Poppa if you could stay with us for a few days until you found a place to rent. And I don't think that I can quite say it the way that he did without being banned indefinitely from DeEtta's mama's house. But the gist of the answer was no," Julia says.

Sandy Earl then comes up with an idea. "If you promise not to touch anything and stay out of sight, you can stay in the shed with the tractor out by the fields," he says.

Marcus, not wanting him to stay anywhere near DeEtta, quickly agrees to take him to get his things and drop him off at the shed. Sandy Earl agrees to ride along with them.

After gathering up Marques's things down by the creek, they head over to the shed. Once there, they unload his few items and put them in the shed. "

Like I said. There shouldn't be anyone coming back here unless they are looking for someone. So try and stay out of sight. I will be by first thing in the morning. Do you have anything to eat?" Sandy Earl asks.

"I'll stay out of sight, I promise. And I got me a few cans of beans, so I'm good. Thank you, I don't know what I would have done if it wasn't for you all," Marques says.

As Marcus and Sandy Earl drive off, the night consumes the area outside the headlamps of Marcus's car as they leave Marques's sight.

"You think that he's going to be okay?" Marcus asks while driving out of the field and back onto the road.

"As long as he doesn't go back up on them Shegogg's front porch. He probably will be just fine," Sandy Earl jokes as he and Marcus laugh until tears run down their faces.

The next day is a Saturday. "Mama, why don't you get ready so I can take you to town when I get back?"

Sandy Earl asks. "I know today is your shopping day, but I promised that guy Marques that I would stop by and check on him this morning. I shouldn't be gone for more than an hour or so." Sandy Earl finishes his breakfast.

While Sandy Earl is gone, Mary tells DeEtta that she needs to keep an eye on her father while she and Sandy Earl run to town. "DeEtta, make sure that he takes his medicine at nine o'clock like he supposed to. If you don't make him, he won't do it. Okay?"

As DeEtta nods her head, Sandy Earl pulls up outside and blows the truck's horn.

"Be sure and check on your father now. We will only be gone for a little while," Mary says as she climbs into the truck. DeEtta closes the door and then makes a cup of tea for Sonny to mix his medicine in. As she walks into her parents' bedroom, she hears her father's heavy, raspy breathing. "Poppa," DeEtta says as she enters the dimly lit room.

Sonny replies in a low whispery voice, "Hi, sweetheart."

DeEtta walks over next to the bed and sits the cup of hot tea on the night table beside his bed. "How are you feeling, Poppa?" she asks.

Sonny replies, "I'm a little tired."

"I brought you some tea. Can I get you anything else, Poppa?" DeEtta asks.

"No...just sit and talk to me if you don't mind," Sonny asks.

"Sure, Poppa! What do you want to talk about?" she asks.

"Are you and Marcus ready for your wedding? I know that I gave him a hard time, but he is a nice young man. And if I don't get a chance to tell him, please tell him that I said so. I just know that you two are going to be so happy," Sonny says.

"Poppa, don't talk like that. You are going to be around to watch all of your grandkids grow up and probably get married," DeEtta says as her eyes start to fill with tears.

"DeEtta, I need for you to do a couple of things for me," Sonny says.

"Anything in the world for you, Poppa," DeEtta replies.

"Promise me that the first opportunity that you and Marcus get, you will move the hell out of Mississippi. Promise me now!" Sonny says.

While her tears are starting to flow, DeEtta says to her father, "We will Poppa!"

Sonny then says, "Tell your mother and brother that I love them so very much and that I'm so...sorry that I couldn't make a better life for all of you." And as Sonny stares off into space, DeEtta says, "I will, Poppa."

And on that chilly spring morning in 1941, while Mary and Sandy Earl are away, Sonny Wells dies.

CHAPTER 18

DeEtta's Day

S ummer 1990—As a warm breeze blows across the open meadow, the slight swaying back and forth of the trees is the only evidence of its existence. For without the presence of the trees or swaying blades of grass, one could think that it came from nowhere and was going nowhere.

"When I'm sad, I try and remember some of the happiest days of my life," Jamil says as the breeze makes its way to the front porch where he and Mama Dee are sitting.

Mama Dee looks at the pictures in a magazine while Jamil licks on an ice cream cone that his mother made for him a little bit ago. Mama Dee smiles as she replies, "How old are you now, thirteen?"

Jamil senses that the question is more about his life experiences and less about his physical age. He answers, "I'm fourteen and will be fifteen on my next birthday."

"I guess a fourteen-year-old could know a little bit about life," Mama Dee replies while still looking at the magazine.

As Stefan comes out onto the porch, Jamil heads into the house to try and talk his mother into giving him another cone of ice cream.

"How are you doing, Mama?" Stefan asks as he sits down next to her.

"I'm doing about as well as a person with my condition can be expected, I suppose," Mama Dee replies.

After a few moments of awkward silence, Mama Dee says to Stefan, "I wanted to tell you as soon as we thought you were old enough to understand. But there never seemed to be a right time to do it...Marcus and I both knew that once we told you, the first question that would have come out of your mouth would have been, 'What happened?' And that was something that Marcus or I just hadn't really come to grips with, let alone ready to try and explain it to our only child."

Stefan then gets up and gives Mama Dee a hug and says, "I think that I need a little more time to get past it. But I'll get past it."

He then kisses Mama Dee on the forehead and goes back into the house. As Mama Dee is sitting by herself, she thinks about what she and Jamil had talked about earlier and decides to take his advice.

* * *

Mid Spring 1941—While Marcus and Sandy Earl unload the truck carrying the food and drink for the wedding, Mary, DeEtta, Mrs. Loo, and Julia hang the decorations.

"It sure is nice of Steven to let us use this hay barn to have the wedding in," Marcus says while carrying a stack of boxes filled with the fried chicken that DeEtta and Mary spent half the night cooking.

"Yes, it is," Sandy Earl replies while helping him with the boxes. After taking the boxes from Marcus, he takes them on inside. Marcus is not allowed inside the barn because DeEtta is in there. And everyone knows that it is bad luck for the groom to see the bride on the day of the wedding prior to her coming down the aisle. So Sandy Earl has been assigned the task of making sure that that doesn't happen.

"Is Marcus still out there?" Julia asks as Sandy Earl sits the boxes on the table.

"Yes, he is. What do you need?" Sandy Earl replies.

"I need you two to go and start getting dressed for the wedding. We are just about done setting up here," Julia tells him.

"Okay, we can do that," he replies while grabbing a couple of pieces of the chicken for the road. He and Marcus then head to Marcus's house to get dressed.

After finishing the decorating, Mary, DeEtta and, Julia head home to do the same. Once they are at the house, DeEtta goes into her brother's room to get dressed while Mary and Julia get dressed in Mary's room. As DeEtta is getting dressed, Mary comes into the room to give her a hand.

"I think that you are going to be the most beautiful bride that anyone on this here place has ever seen," Mary says as she brushes DeEtta's hair.

"Thanks, Mama!" DeEtta replies.

DeEtta then takes a deep breath and exhales before saying what has been on both of their minds all week. "I sure wish Poppa was here," DeEtta says as she stares into the mirror, looking at her mother's reflection.

Mary, while trying not to make eye contact with DeEtta, doesn't reply. In her mind, words of strength and encouragement are there. But in her heart, she knows that if she starts to speak of Sonny, she will simply break down and start to cry like she has done almost every night since the day that he died. And that is something that she doesn't want her daughter dealing with on her wedding day. So, instead of replying to what DeEtta has said, Mary starts to hum her favorite church song. DeEtta hums right along with her mother.

After getting dressed, Marcus and Sandy Earl head back over to the hay barn. Once they arrive, Marcus is eager to see what it looks like inside since he wasn't allowed in while they were doing the decorating. As he walks through the door, he is amazed at how Mary, Julia, Sandy Earl, and DeEtta have transformed the place.

They have aligned several arbors all in a row, creating a tunnel, and dressed them all up with ribbons and flowers. And as he walks through the arbors, he is led to a semicircle made from stacked bales of hay with an altar setting in its center. The place looks as if they have harvested every spring flower in the county and used them to decorate it.

Bales of hay have been lined up in rows for seating with ribbon bows on each row's end. The altar is set up were when the sunlight shines through the upper doors of the barn; it will shine down upon it like a beacon from the heavens above. The main table for the food is also made with stacked bales of hay and covered with some of Mrs. Loo's finest linen, which Mary purchased with some of the money that she and Sonny had been saving up for a place of their own.

I could not have imagined a more beautiful place to get married in, Marcus thinks while standing next to the altar and trying to take it all in.

Shortly after Marcus and Sandy Earl get situated, the guests start to arrive. The first to show up is Ms. Lillie and the two ladies she sits next to in church. And before long, the place is almost filled to its capacity. Marcus, Sandy Earl, and Rev. Mitchel wait out back as Marques ushers the people to their seats.

"Are you ready for this, almost brother-in-law?" Sandy Earl asks.

"I've been ready for this ever since I first laid my eyes on your sister," Marcus replies with a big grin on his face. And with that, Marcus and Rev. Mitchel enter the building while Sandy Earl heads around to the front to walk in with his sister.

After standing up at the altar for what seems like forever, Marcus and Rev. Mitchel start to get the feeling that something might be wrong. And just as Marcus is about to excuse himself to go and find out what has happened, Sandy Earl walks in through the back door and whispers in his ear, "Mama and DeEtta are not here yet. Give me your car keys so that I can run to the house and check on them," Sandy Earl asks.

Rev. Mitchel then announces to the waiting crowd, "The wedding has been delayed for a little bit, and it should be starting soon."

Marcus tells Sandy Earl that he wants to ride along with him. And as both of them are getting into Marcus's car, Steven Shegogg's car pulls up in front of the barn with Julia, Mary, and DeEtta inside. Sandy Earl quickly tells Marcus to go back inside the church so that he doesn't see the bride before the wedding.

Sandy Earl is happy to see that his mother and sister are okay but confused and puzzled to see them all riding in Steven's car. "What happened?" Sandy Earls asks.

"During all of the excitement leading up to the wedding, we forgot to put gas in the truck. Steven saw that we were having problems and offered to give us a ride," DeEtta replies.

Sandy Earl looks over at Steven and says, "Thanks!"

And as Steven starts to walk away, DeEtta says, "I just know that are coming to our wedding. Aren't you?"

Steven smiles and says, "Are you sure that you want a Shegogg at your wedding?"

DeEtta replies, "Not just any Shegogg, but Steven Shegogg is more than welcome."

Steven then walks into the barn and takes a seat in the back so that he doesn't cause a commotion.

Soon after everyone is in their places, the wedding begins. Sandy Earl first walks Mary down the aisle and sits her up front. They are followed by little Irma Jean, who is the flower girl.

Irma Jean's father smiles, and her mother cries as she passes them while scattering rose petals onto the floor as she makes her way down the aisle. After the flower girl has covered the path to the altar with rose petals, there is a brief yet sweet silence as the entire gathering awaits the entering of the bride. The doors slowly open, and there stands Sandy Earl and his beautiful sister, DeEtta.

As Sandy Earl walks his sister down the aisle, his mind is filled with many thoughts. He remembers his father and all of the sacrifices that he had made for them. He thinks about his mother and the sacrifices that she continues to make. He also thinks about his sister, whom he loves dearly.

As the tears of joy flow from her eyes, DeEtta looks up at her brother and thanks him for being there for her as he gives her hand to Marcus. Marcus also thanks Sandy Earl for being a friend and now a brother-in-law. And as Rev. Mitchel broadcasts the oaths of matrimony, Marcus and DeEtta gaze profoundly into one another's eyes.

Rev. Mitchel then asks Marcus, "Do you take this woman for your wife until death do you part?"

Marcus replies, "I will, with all my heart and soul."

Rev. Mitchel then asks DeEtta the same question, and she replies, "I will, with every beat of my heart."

He then pronounces them husband and wife. After saluting his bride, Marcus and DeEtta pay honor a tradition that has signified the nuptial of African Americans since slavery as they both jump across the broom.

After parading around in the barn several times, DeEtta tosses her bouquet into the air. And as the bouquet flies through the air with its streamers of ribbon waving at the unlucky would-be captors as it passes over them, the crowd cheers. It finds itself a new home in the arms of Ms. Lillie. The crowd bursts into laughter as they congratulate her for the great catch.

Before the partying starts, Julia raises a glass of cheer to her lifelong friend DeEtta and her newly wedded husband Marcus. Although her words are short, DeEtta feels each and every one of them as she listens to what her friend has to say.

With tears flowing, Julia says, "To my lifelong friend. May her marriage be filled with love, understanding, and a type of longevity that not only measures time but also measures the depth of the love that DeEtta and Marcus have for one another."

As everyone drinks from their cups, Steven looks over at Julia and smiles.

The wedding party goes on until the early hours of the morning. And as the sun's morning rays burn away the early morning mist that hovers over the creek and fields that line its banks, the last of the guests leave for home.

"That sure was one heck of a wedding," Marques says to Sandy Earl as they close the party down and start to pick up the trash that is left behind.

"Yes, it sure was," Sandy Earl replies.

Later that day, after getting some rest. Marcus and DeEtta, who now live with Marcus and his parents, stop by Mary's house to see if they need to help clean up after the wedding.

"We got it, brother-in-law," Sandy Earl replies while still wearing the suit that he wore to the wedding.

Mary, who has just gotten out of bed, makes her way into the kitchen. "How are the newlyweds doing this fine afternoon?" Mary asks as she pours herself a cup of coffee.

"We're doing wonderfully, Mama," DeEtta replies while displaying a huge grin on her face.

Mary smiles as she sees the look of happiness blossoming across her daughter's face. "So what are your plans for today?" Mary asks.

"We were thinking about going to talk to Mr. Shegogg to see if he has a larger place that we could maybe rent. Marcus's parents' place is barely large enough for them and Marcus," DeEtta says.

Mary then asks Sandy Earl, DeEtta, and Marcus to take a seat at the table while she fixes them all a late breakfast. While they are all sitting at the table, Mary places a skillet onto the stove to heat up, and she starts breaking eggs and putting them into a bowl. She asks, "Why don't you guys move in here?"

"Where would we all sleep?" DeEtta asks.

"Well…I thought that you and Marcus can sleep in my room, and Sandy Earl can stay in his," Mary says.

"And where are you going to sleep, Mama?" DeEtta asks.

"Well…I received a letter from Betty the other day, and we were thinking that maybe, with Sonny and Ed both being gone…She was wondering if I could maybe move to California and live with her. She has a three-bedroom house, and the only other thing that lives with her is her cat," Mary answers. "And besides, every time I walk through that door, I catch myself listening for Sonny's voice. And each and every time that I don't hear it, it feels as if a little bit more of me fades away. Plus, now that both of you are grown and hopefully will be starting families of your own, it would be a lot easier on you two if you didn't have to worry about me.

"I love the both of you with all that I have within my soul. And I want to give y'all the best chance that I can for you to make it in this world. I owe that much to Sonny! Because the Lord knows that man did everything that he could to give you two a chance in this world," Mary adds as she continues to crack eggs.

DeEtta and Sandy Earl both sit silently as they digest what their mother is telling them. After thinking about for a moment, DeEtta says, "Mama, you're not keeping us from doing anything. And if you move all the way to California, how will we ever see you again?"

Mary answers, "DeEtta, I have been on this here place ever since I was born. My mother, your grandmother, lived and worked on this place pretty much all of her life. Baby, it's time!" Mary then removes the skillet from the heat and goes back into her bedroom and closes the door.

The following Sunday, DeEtta, and Julia sit in their regular seats behind Ms. Lillie and her gossiping buddies. But on this Sunday, it was a little different. They are joined by Marcus.

Before the start of service, Ms. Lillie says to one of her friends sitting next to her, "Child! I don't know what Mrs. Shegogg is going to do if the mister dies. Everybody in the house knows that he is sick with cancer. That's why nobody hasn't seen him out and about. And them two boys of theirs hate one another so much that—and I truly believe—if it wasn't for Mr. Shegogg, that John Jr. would probably kill his brother, Steven."

Marcus, DeEtta, and Julia can't help but hear what is being said as they sit there less than a few feet away. However, once again, they pretend that they don't.

As Rev. Mitchel steps into the pulpit, the church is asked to rise. "Good morning, church!" the reverend says.

The church then replies, "Good morning!"

"The reason that I asked all of you to stand this morning is that I just want to give an acknowledgment to our church's newest family. Everyone, please put your hands together for Mr. and Mrs. Marcus Lee Waters."

As the entire church claps their hands, Marcus and DeEtta waves to everyone.

By the end of the service, there are two very significant stories circulating among the congregation. The first is about Mr. Shegogg being on his death bed. And the other is about Mary moving off to California.

DeEtta and Julia have not seen this level of gossiping since the levee break and the mud slide that followed.

"So, is your mother really moving away to California?" Ms. Lillie asks DeEtta after practically breaking her neck to catch her before she and Marcus can make it to their car.

"There she is, ask her yourself," DeEtta replies as she looks over at Mary, who is standing behind Ms. Lillie.

Mary replies to the question before Ms. Lillie can get over the shock of her having been standing right behind her while she was trying to put her nose clearly where it didn't belong. "My family and I are talking about it."

Mary then walks on past and gets into the truck with Sandy Earl.

CHAPTER 19

Change

Summer 1990—"I'm sure glad that you are feeling better," Jamil says to Mama Dee after finally being able to talk her into taking a ride on the golf cart with him.

"Now, if you can just slow this thing down a little bit, maybe this won't be the last time that I'll take a ride with you," Mama Dee says as she cringes while leaning into the turn as they come flying around the house.

Seeing that Mama Dee is not comfortable or impressed with his high-G turns and instantaneous ability to accelerate, Jamil slows down as they head off in the direction of the front gate.

"Hey Mama Dee, would you like to see the really old car that I found parked in the old barn that's on the other side of the cemetery?" Jamil asks as they are driving alone.

"Sure! Why not," Mama Dee answers.

After the drive down the stone path through the cemetery, they come upon an old rickety barn. Although the barn is in disrepair with its roof collapsing on one side, this structure Mama Dee knew well from the days of the

Harvest Festivals. Jamil stops the cart and walks around to the other side to help Mama Dee out.

"It's right in here," Jamil says as he lifts and pushes one of the leaning doors open.

Mama Dee gasps as she gazes upon the black 1940 Ford automobile. With three of its tires pretty much rotted away while still on the rims and the fourth tire and wheel missing altogether, Mama Dee knows well who this car once belonged to.

"Come on let's go!" She says to Jamil.

While riding back through the cemetery, Mama Dee doesn't say a word. Sensing that the reason for her silence could be because of something that he said or done, Jamil tries to strike up a conversation by asking, "So does any of this look familiar to you, Mama Dee?" as they drive pass the row of now dilapidated shacks that line the road leading to the main house.

"Stop the cart!" Mama Dee says.

Jamil slams on the brakes so hard that he and Mama Dee both have to catch themselves as they are pushed forward from the momentum as the cart slides to a stop.

After regaining her composure, Mama Dee calmly says to Jamil, "If you do that again, one of us will be walking back to the house! And it won't be me. Got it?"

Jamil replies to Mama Dee with a solemn, "Yes, ma'am!"

Mama Dee then gets off the cart once more and walks over to one of the shacks. "Right here is where your great grandparents, Sonny and Mary Wells, and my brother Sandy Earl and I all stayed," she says.

"All four of you guys stayed in that tiny house?" Jamil asks in disbelief.

"Yes, we did. And were damn glad to have had it back then. The house that we stayed in before we moved into this one was about half that size. It had only two rooms; my parents slept in the front room, and my brother and I slept on the floor of the other, which was also the kitchen," Mama Dee explains to him. She then adds while pointing up at the hills, "The first house got washed away in a mudslide. Your great, great grandparents on your grandfather's side lived and died there. And it was where your grandfather was born."

Mama Dee and Jamil then get back on the cart and continue their trip toward the front gate. After pulling up to the gate, Jamil turns the cart around and heads back toward the house. As the cart starts to climb the hill, the battery goes dead. Jamil is able to let it roll back down the hill and park it under a large maple tree so that Mama Dee is out of the sun.

"Okay, Mama Dee, you sit right here. I'm going to walk back up to the house and get Mama to bring the car down for you," Jamil explains as he takes charge of the situation.

Mama Dee, knowing that the house is less than a half of a mile away, smiles and shakes her head in agreement. Jamil then starts his journey back to the house. While he is gone, Mama Dee sits back on the cart's seat and watches him as he walks past the row of rundown shacks. She then looks up toward the house as Jamil disappears from her sight.

After sitting there for a while looking up the road, she starts to think about her father, Sonny, her mother, Mary, and her brother, Sandy Earl. And she tries to remember the last time that all of them slept under the same roof. For the life of her, she cannot recall that day. Instead, her mind leads her to remembers a different day.

* * *

Early Summer 1941—As Sandy Earl turns onto the dirt road leading to their house, he sees more than the usual amount of people standing out in front of their house talking. No sooner has he parked than one of the neighbors walks up to the truck.

"What's going on, Mr. Davis?" Sandy Earl asks as he is getting out of the truck.

"I guess you haven't heard yet. Sam's boy came over from the mill a little while ago and said that he saw a funeral car up at the Shegogg's place."

Sandy Earl knows that if what he is hearing is true, it probably means that Mr. Shegogg has passed away. And for Sandy Earl and every other sharecropper who worked and lived on the Shegogg's place, it was a bittersweet pill to swallow. The sweetness is that one of the most feared and hated white men in Mississippi has died. The bitterness is that the only person who is more hated than he is his son John Jr., who might now very well be the person in charge of everything.

As the verification of Big John's death comes to pass, an almost eerie feeling of mourning falls over the place. The sentiment is not being generated out of sorrow, empathy, or pity for the Shegogg family. It is being generated out of fear. And that fear is of the unknown.

DeEtta, Marcus, Sandy Earl, and Mary sit at the dinner table, wondering what course of action should they take, if any.

"Well, there's not really a lot that any of us sharecroppers can do because we have already planted for the season," Sandy Earl says after giving the situation some thought.

Marcus agrees with him and adds, "We would all be fools playing right into John Jr.'s hands if we just left our crops and walked away. All he would need to do is hire someone to harvest them. And as hard as times are out here, it wouldn't cost much and most of us would lose whatever little we have. Especially those of us that owe them money."

After having the conversation, they agree to several things. The first is they will stay and see how things play out. Another is as soon as they could get things set up, Mary will be leaving to go stay with her sister in California. And the last is Marcus and DeEtta will be moving in with Sandy Earl after Mary leaves.

Throughout the following days, wealthy and important white folks are seen coming to and leaving the Shegogg's house. But the now matriarch to the Shegogg empire, Kathy May Shegogg, who was often seen sitting on her bedroom balcony looking out over the place as if she were the eyes watching from the heavens above, is rarely seen during the whole grieving process.

As the day of the funeral draws near, John Jr. becomes more and more involved in the day-to-day running of the cotton gin and warehouse. Steven has taken to running the store and rental property business.

"Good morning, Steven," Julia says as she walks into the store. Steven is in the process of showing one of his workers how to put together one of the new sales displays that had been delivered earlier that morning.

"Good morning, Julia," Steven replies.

"I heard about your father, and my heart goes out to you," Julia says as Steven stops what he is doing and walks over to where she is standing.

"It's very nice to hear you say that. But you didn't really have to because you know as well as I do he was a living and breathing son of a bitch. And yes, I am sad that he is gone, but not for the reason that you think," Steven replies.

Julia isn't shocked in the slightest by what Steven has said. During their many surreptitious meetings, the conversation about how he felt about his father had come up often. "I didn't say that I was sorry that he was dead. I said that my heart goes out to you. Even though you didn't care much for him, he was still your father. And I know that with his passing, there is a burden being put on you," Julia replies.

"I'm just about done here. If you want, I could give you a ride home," Steven says.

Julia replies, "Big John might be dead, but the rest of Mississippi and Jim Crow are still very much alive and kicking. I think it would be best if I walked."

Steven stops and shakes his head and smiles as Julia walks back out the door and heads toward home.

Sandy Earl stops by the warehouse to pick up a bundle of cotton sacks while on his way home. As he walks through the door, he notices that John Jr. has hired several of his drinking buddies at the warehouse.

"What the hell do you want, nigger?" Sandy Earl is asked by one of the new employees as he walks up to the counter.

But before Sandy Earl can answer, one of the older employees says, "How are you doing this morning, Sandy Earl? I'll take care of you over here."

As Sandy Earl walks over to the other counter, John Jr.'s friend glares at the older employee as if he wants to say something about him interfering in what was happening. The older employee stares right back at him and asks the question, "Is there a problem?"

John Jr.'s friend then looks off in a different direction. Sandy Earl is somewhat surprised because he and his father have been called even harsher names by the same employee who has now come to his defense.

One does not need to be a rocket scientist to see that the older employees aren't happy with the changes that have taken place at the gin or the warehouse. Although Big John had only been dead for a few days, the animosity between the old and the new has already started to fester. After getting what he came for, Sandy Earl heads back to his truck. As he is getting ready to pull off, he sees Julia walking down the road. "Need a ride?" he asks.

"Sure!" Julia replies.

As they are riding along, Sandy Earl asks Julia about Steven. "I saw you talking to Steven when I drove through town earlier. How is he doing?"

"He's doing okay, I suppose," Julia replies.

"You two guys have become pretty good friends from what I hear," Sandy Earl says.

"It's not what you think, Sandy Earl!" Julia replies.

"Now, what is it that I might be thinking?" Sandy Earl asks. "Julia, I have known you your whole life, and I love you almost as much I love my little sister DeEtta. And if it looks like something is going on between you two to me, what in the world do you think the other people are seeing? They have eyes too! And for the life of me, I am not trying to get into your business, but I do care about you. So I'm just saying. This is Mississippi, and you need to be mindful of what some of the people around here think," Sandy Earl adds.

Julia doesn't say another word for the rest of the time that they are driving. She just gazes out the window and tries to keep from showing that her feelings are hurt. After dropping Julia off at her house, Sandy Earl drives out to the field to check on the tractor before heading home.

On the morning of Big John's funeral, the rain falls as if it is being poured from the heavens with buckets, and the road to the Shegogg's family cemetery is all but washed out. Mrs. Shegogg orders that the funeral procession drive through the center of town and pass the row of houses with their name written across their roof tops before heading to the cemetery.

And as the procession makes its way down through the center of town, the rain is falling so heavy, and the wind is blowing so hard that there is no one lining the streets and showing their respect as Mrs. Shegogg hoped to see. Those who wanted to watch the procession can only do so from the windows of the business on Main Street or through the windows of their houses.

After leaving town, the procession heads for the Shegogg's estate. As it proceeds down the two-lane road, the rain and the wind start to slow and eventually stop just as the procession pulls through the gates. The procession then makes its way up the hill toward the row of tiny houses. And as Mrs. Shegogg looks through the window of the limousine, she is taken aback by the sheer number of Black people who have lined the road and are standing out in front of the minuscule structures.

Some were soaking wet, and others have their feet covered with mud. It is as if they had walked a great distance as the rain was falling. And many of them are so poor that they have no shoes and only rags to wear for clothing. But still, they came to see.

And the one single thing that Mrs. Shegogg will remember most about this day and probably take to her grave is the looks on their faces. Although there is no cheering, laughing, or dancing, the looks on their faces are not the ones of grief she had wanted so badly for someone other than herself to feel and outwardly display. Instead, she sees a gathering of people looking to witness for themselves that a true tyrant has died and hopefully will be judged for his actions and deeds come judgment day.

DeEtta, Marcus, Mary, and Sandy Earl watch from their front porch as the hearse drives past. Julia and Marques stand quietly next to one another among the large crowd of spectators. After passing the row of shacks, the procession then turns and goes down the dirt road leading to the Shegogg's family cemetery.

As the crowd starts to disperse, Sandy Earl says, "Things are about to get really crazy around here."

Marcus asks, "What do you mean by that?"

Sandy Earl then tells them all about what had happened when he had gone to the warehouse to pick up the cotton sacks. "You should have seen the way that they looked at one another. It was as if they not only didn't trust one another, but they didn't care for each other in the least. Don't know what kind of deal Big John had worked out with the older guys. But it looks like old John Jr. and his friends are rocking the boat. And I sure hope that we don't get caught up in the middle of it," Sandy Earl answers.

That night, the lights at the Shegogg house stay on until the next day. Thus, Sandy Earl can pretty much see anyone who walks past a window as he sits on the front porch puffing on his father's old corn cob pipe. As the symphony of crickets brings their early night concert to a close, a hoot owl and several coyotes send their calls of approval echoing through the valley as he watches Mrs. Shegogg come out onto her balcony and sit for only a few minutes and then go back inside. After watching her repeat the process several times, it becomes obvious that she is unable to find comfort in her own space.

How could someone who has so much have so little? Sandy Earl wonders as he takes a puff from the pipe.

CHAPTER 20

Parting of Ways

Summer 1990—"Mama Dee, I would have been willing to bet money that you had more sense than to get on that golf cart with that boy. Stefan is going to be pissed when he finds out," Clarice says while giving Jamil the evil eye.

"It not his fault that I got on that cart. And the only thing that happened was that the darn battery went dead. It's not as if anyone got hurt or anything," Mama Dee replies.

Jamil smiles at Mama Dee when Clarice turns and looks at the road as she drives them back up to the house.

"And I really don't see why you need to say anything to Stefan about this. Especially if you think it's going to upset him. Because he is going to be upset a plenty because my grandson and I will be taking some more rides together. And there is nothing that he can do to stop it. I believe that I am a grown-ass woman, and it's not up to you guys if I ride on a damn cart or not!" Mama Dee says after the car has stopped and she is getting out. "Come on, Jamil, let's take a walk," Mama Dee says as she walks toward the flower garden.

Jamil looks over at his mother before moving an inch.

"Go ahead, get out of here. But you better let one of us know before you ever take her anywhere on that cart again," Clarice says as he gets out of the car.

"Yes, I promise I will, Mama," Jamil says as he hops out the car with a big smile on his face and scurries off to catch up to Mama Dee.

"Mama Dee, did the people who lived in this house when you were growing up have any children?" Jamil asks while walking and looking at the flowers with Mama Dee.

"Yes, they had two boys. Steven and John Jr. They were as different as day and night," Mama Dee answers.

"Did you guys ever play with them?" Jamil asks.

"Oh no. You see, back then in the South, Black kids and white kids were not allowed to play together. Especially on this here place," Mama Dee replies.

After walking a little father, Jamil asks, "Mama Dee, you said earlier that my great grandfather Sonny died in that little house back there. What happened to my great grandmother?" Mama Dee sits down on one of the benches that she had Stefan put in the garden after they had planted the flowers and asks Jamil to sit down beside her. She then explains why his great grandmother died someplace other than the little shack that his great grandfather had died in.

* * *

Mid-Summer 1941—The intense rays from the sun distribute a blistering heat on the backs of Sandy Earl,

Marques, and the numerous other field workers as they dot the landscape of the immense valley while preforming the gruesome, labor-intense task of weeding and thinning out the cotton plants. This task is called "chopping cotton".

"These rows look like they never end," Marques, who had never had the opportunity or need to perform such a chore before, says to Sandy Earl as he works in the row of cotton next to him.

Sandy Earl smiles and grunts as an acknowledgment of what Marques has stated.

"How could anyone do this every day?" Marques asks as he removes his hat and leans on the handle of his hoe. He then pulls his handkerchief from his pocket and wipes the sweat from his face.

"I suppose if you have never done this before, it does take some getting used to," Sandy Earl replies as he continues to look down at the cotton plants as he weeds and thins them out. After not hearing a reply back from Marques, Sandy Earl stops and looks back over his shoulder. Marques is lying face down in the dirt with his handkerchief still in his hand.

About twenty minutes later, Marques wakes up and finds himself lying under a large shade tree at the edge of the field. His shirt is sopping wet from someone pouring water on him to cool him off. And on the ground next to him sits a bucket of water with a ladle in it. Marques takes a drink from the bucket and stands on his feet. After knocking the dust from his clothes, he looks around for Sandy Earl.

Sandy Earl can be seen off in the far distance, still working in the field as if nothing had happened. After seeing Sandy Earl, Marques makes his way back out into the field and retrieves his hat and hoe. He then picks up where he left off without either of them saying a word.

As the sun makes its exit, a soothing gust of wind sweeps across the open fields. The comforting breeze feels as if it is a godsend. With its gentle touch, it caresses the necks and backs of all who had remained loyal to the task.

While coming in from the field, Sandy Earl asks Marques, "Are you okay?"

Marques replies with a simple nodding of his head while continuing to stare straight ahead, too exhausted to speak or even look in another direction. After making it to the shed, Marques plops down on one of the large logs that Sandy Earl has placed around the front side of the shed for seating.

Sandy Earl goes into the shed and retrieves his bastard file and sits down on the log across from Marques. As he starts to sharpen the edge of his hoe in preparation for the next day in the field, he asks Marques, "I believe you told me that you were from Philadelphia? Are the rest of your family still there?"

Marques replies, "My mother and little sister are. Not sure where my father is. I only saw him once when I was a child. It was back when I was seven years old. He walked up to me one day and said, 'Your mama tells me that I'm your father.' After taking a close look at me, he said, 'I think that she is just trying to get some money from me.

Because you don't look a damn thing like me!' He then turned and walked away.

"Some years later, when I was eighteen years old, a lady claiming to be his sister came to see my mother and me. She said that some jealous husband had caught him with his wife and had shot him in the back as he was trying to run. He was in the hospital, and it was looking like he wasn't going to make it.

"You wouldn't believe what she said next. She said that he told her, 'It would be good if I could see my only son again before he died.' I told her to tell him the same thing that he told me back when I was seven: 'I think that he just trying to get somebody to come and see him. Because he doesn't look a damn thing like me.' And that was the last I heard of him," Marques concludes.

"By the way, how old are you?" Sandy Earl asks.

"I'll be twenty-six on my next birthday. And in that short period time, I have hoboed on trains from Minnesota to Mississippi. I have seen both of the oceans. I have walked past the White House, and I've fished for crabs in the San Francisco bay. I have slept on some of the most prestigious streets in this here country," Marques replies as they both laugh. "Have you been anywhere other than Mississippi?" Marques asks Sandy Earl.

"To be perfectly honest with you, Marques, I have never crossed the state line. Hell, I've only been outside of this here county twice," Sandy Earl replies as he momentarily stops filing on the hoe as the reality of what he has just said sinks in.

"The way I look at it, life is too short to worry about the things that you can't control. I don't have a damn thing and probably never will. But in the end, I would have seen more than all of these sons of bitches down here put together. And that is something that no matter what happens, nobody can take it away from me," Marques says. He then stands up, stretches, and goes around to the back of the shed to use the bathroom.

After putting away the tools, Sandy Earl asks Marques, "Do I need to bring you some food or anything when I come back tomorrow?"

Marques replies with a smile on his face, "Yeah, one of the pretty girls to keep me warm at night would be nice."

"I think that might be something that you would be better off taking care of yourself. See you tomorrow morning, and drink plenty of water tonight. Tomorrow is going to be another hot one," Sandy Earl replies as he gets in his truck and drives off.

On his way home, Sandy Earl stops by Bo's house to see DeEtta and Marcus. As he pulls up to the house, he sees Bo and Marcus outside working on Marcus's car.

"How is it going this evening?" Sandy Earl asks.

"It will be going a lot better once I get this damn clutch adjusted," Marcus replies as he gets up off on the ground and walks over to Sandy Earl's truck.

"Is DeEtta home? I need to talk with her about Mama's going-away party," Sandy Earl says.

"She is in the house helping Nancy cook dinner. Are you going to stay and eat with us?" Marcus asks.

"I would love to, but I need to head home because Mama will be looking for me. And she probably already done fixed something," Sandy Earl replies.

"So, y'all's mama is really going to move to California?" Bo asks.

"Yep, that's the plan," Sandy Earl replies.

After hearing all the back and forth chatter coming from outside, DeEtta comes to the door. "How are you doing, big brother?" DeEtta asks as she walks over to the truck and gives Sandy Earl a hug. "How is Mama doing?" she asks.

"We are doing just fine. I stopped by so we can start working out some of the details for her surprise going-away party," Sandy Earl says.

"There is not a whole lot left to work out. Julia said that she is going to give me a hand with the food. All I need for you to do is make sure that you take her to town Saturday morning like you always do, and make sure you keep her there until eleven o'clock. We are going to take care of the rest," DeEtta says.

"Sounds like a plan. And with that, I guess that I'll be seeing all of you on Saturday then," Sandy Earl says before starting the truck.

As the moon fades away and the dew of the new morning covers every surface that is exposed to the coming light of day, Sandy Earl pulls up in front of the shed out at the fields. The sound of the truck's engine awakens Marques as he slept underneath the rear axle of the tractor.

"Good morning. I brought you some coffee and an egg sandwich. The coffee might even still be warm," Sandy Earl says as he gets out of the truck and hands Marques the old jelly jar with the coffee in it and the sandwich.

Marques stretches and replies, "You sure know the way to a man's heart." After Marques finishes his breakfast, they both gather up their tools and head back in the fields.

After working for several long hours, Sandy Earl says to Marques, "I need to run into town to take care of something. Do you want to ride along with me?"

"Sure! Anything to get out of this hot sun for a little bit," Marques replies.

Once they make it to town, Sandy Earl pulls up in front of the Mr. and Mrs. Loo's store.

"You can sit here in the truck if you want. I need to go inside and talk to Mrs. Loo about my mother's party. I won't be long," Sandy Earl says as he gets out of the truck.

While sitting in the truck, Marques rolls himself a cigarette and starts people watching while puffing on it. After sitting there for only a short while waiting, he notes how much more segregated the deep South is than the rest of the country.

The whites are going about their daily lives of shopping, taking morning walks with their dogs, and sitting on the benches in front of the town hall while engaging in conversation, while everyone else looks to be doing everything they can to steer clear of them. He watches a white man and his wife come upon an elderly Black woman while walking down the sidewalk. The elderly Black woman steps into the road as they approach her. It was as if they don't even see her. Yet she knew that it was in her best interest to simply get out of their way.

Everywhere he looks, he sees how the people of color are systematically practicing avoidance. They turn the corner or cross the street rather than simply walk past. And at all costs, they avoid direct eye contact. Having traveled as much as he has, Marques knows firsthand that the other parts of the country had their issues with race as well. But here, he feels it is so much different.

"This is something that you not only see everywhere that you look, but you feel it everywhere you go. It is as if you can taste it with every breath that you inhale. You unconsciously think about it each night before you lay down to sleep. And you awaken to its present, each morning as you opened your eyes. It is as if it was your shadow, and it stays with you everywhere that you go.

"It's as obvious as the leaves on the trees or the sun while it sits high in the sky over the cotton fields. Yet, everyone goes about their daily lives as if it is nothing ominous." he reasons. It is then that Marques realizes that here in the Mississippi Delta is not where he wants to spend any more time than he has already spent.

After Sandy Earl finishes his business with Mrs. Loo, he walks back out to his truck. And when he gets there, Marques is nowhere in sight. On the dashboard of the truck, he finds a note that reads, *Dear friend, I want to thank you, your family, and Julia for allowing me the opportunity to witness what a real family and having true friends is really like. Hopefully, one day I too will have the same, Marques.*

On the day of the party, Sandy Earl and Mary head to town a little earlier than usual. Mary is in a hurry to get there to buy some new material to make herself a couple of new dresses before leaving for California. It is also the first weekend of the month, which is when

Mrs. Loo puts out her new material and puts some of the old material on sale. And Mary wants to get there before it gets picked over.

While Sandy Earl and Mary are away in town, Marcus, DeEtta, and Julia work on getting the house ready for the party. DeEtta baked a cake and made some corn muffins earlier that morning. Julia cooked a big pot of greens and helped DeEtta with the cutting up and the frying of the chicken the night before.

"After you get done bringing in those chairs, you can run back up to the house and pick up Papa Bo and Mama Nancy, if you don't mind," DeEtta says to Marcus.

After Marcus leaves, DeEtta looks for Julia, who was standing in the kitchen a little bit ago. After walking through the house and not finding her, DeEtta goes around to the back of the house, which is where she finds her. Julia is throwing up on the ground.

"Are you okay?" DeEtta asks.

"Yes, I am now," Julia replies as she finishes. "I have really been feeling sick to my stomach here lately. Not sure what's going on. It comes, and it goes," Julia says as they both walk back around to the front of the house.

After cleaning herself up, Julia helps DeEtta with the finishing touches. As the guests start to arrive, Marcus instructs them to park their cars, wagons, and mules down the road and at the neighbors' houses so that Mary won't suspect anything. And at eleven o'clock on the button, Sandy Earl's truck makes the turn at the bottom of the hill. As the truck pulls up in front of the house, the only living things standing out in front of the row of houses are a couple of chickens and the old blue tick hound dog named Rex.

Sandy Earl tells Mary to go ahead on inside while he gets the bags out of the truck. As Mary opens the door, she is greeted with a loud, heartfelt *"Surprise!"*

Mary immediately breaks down and starts to cry. And as her friends hug her and wish her well in the new phase of her life, she tells each and every one of them how much they will be missed and promises to try her best to come back to see them all someday.

As the celebration continues on into the late afternoon, Mary is presented with a gift from her two children and son-in-law. DeEtta hands her mother a box wrapped in store-bought wrapping paper with a pink ribbon tied around it. Mary is speechless as she accepts and opens the gift. After opening it, Mary starts crying all over again. They are her first brand-new, store-bought dresses. And there are three of them.

And as the party ends and the people start to leave, Mary stops Mrs. Loo as she is heading to her car and says to her, "You know what? Out of all the people around here that I'm going to miss, I think that it will be you that I'm going to miss the most. I'm not sure if it's because of the forever welcoming smiles you gave me whenever I came into your store. Or if it's because of the warm and meaningful conversations that we have shared through the years. Either way, I'm am going to truly miss you."

Mrs. Loo removes her glasses, wipes her eyes, and says, "A truer friend I have never had." She then gets into the car with her husband and drives off.

Three days later, Sandy Earl, Marcus, and DeEtta take Mary to the train station.

"Well, I guess this is it," DeEtta says to her mother as they are all standing alongside the train with its engine running and the smell of diesel fuel in the air.

"If you all don't do anything else that I asked you to do, promise me one thing? That you guys will be sure and take care of one another. Because family is all we ever had. And it's the only thing that they couldn't take away from us," Mary says before giving DeEtta a hug.

Mary then walks over to Sandy Earl. "Look at my boy! Standing here looking just like his daddy…"

Before she can finish what she is saying, Sandy Earl gives his mother the biggest bear hug that she can stand as tears fall from his face.

And with that, the conductor calls out, "All aboard!" and Mary is helped onto the train. A couple of minutes later, the train pulls off.

CHAPTER 21

Brothers

Late Summer 1990—Clarice helps Mama Dee from the wheelchair and onto the bed after helping her to remove her sweater and shoes. Mama Dee thanks her as she lies back and stretches out on the bed. Clarice then covers her with a blanket.

"These treatments are getting harder and harder to bounce back from," Mama Dee says while lying there with her eyes closed.

"Can I get you anything?" Clarice asks.

"No, I think I'm good for right now," Mama Dee replies.

"Why don't you try and get some rest? I'll come back and check on you later," Clarice says as she walks toward the door. As Clarice leaves the room, she leaves the door partly open so that they can hear if Mama Dee calls out for something.

While lying in bed, Mama Dee's mind wanders for only a short while before she falls off to sleep. While she is sleeping, Clarice and Stefan come back into the room to check on her. While in there, they sit down beside her bed and say a short prayer for her to get better.

"You do know that you mean the world to her, don't you?" Clarice whispers to Stefan.

"Yeah! I know," Stefan replies.

"Well, don't you think it is about time that you two get over what happened in the past and move forward?" Clarice asks. "Life is too short," she adds.

Stefan nods his head in agreement as they both leave the room.

After a few hours have passed, Stefan comes back up to the room carrying a sandwich and some soup. "Come on, sleepyhead, it's time to wake up and eat something. It will make you feel a whole lot better," Stefan says as he enters the room. Mama Dee opens her eyes and sits up in the bed while he adjusts her pillows.

"So are you feeling a little bit sick or a lot of sick?" Stefan jokingly asks.

"A little bit sick. Why do you ask?" Mama Dee replies.

"Because if you were a lot a sick, I was going to feed you. But being that you are a little bit sick, you can feed yourself," he answers.

As Mama Dee forces down as much food as she can, Stefan sits beside her bed and keeps her company. After realizing that no one is doing much talking and that the long periods of silence have become obviously awkward, Mama Dee says, "You are sitting here like you want to ask me something that you are either too afraid to or not sure that you want to hear the answer that I might give you. Go ahead, ask. What's on your mind, son?" She then sits the half-empty bowl of soup down on the tray.

"Can you tell me if I was a surprise or was I something that was planned?" Stefan asks.

Mama Dee adjusts herself about the bed as she starts to collect her thoughts. After a brief hesitation, she asks Stefan, "I guess the question that you are really asking is was there love for you before you were born?" She then clears her throat and says, "There was a lot going on back then," before going on to tell him about when they found out that he was coming into this world.

* * *

Late Summer 1941—There is a loud banging at the front door. Marcus jumps out of bed and grabs his pants and puts them on while running to answer it. As he comes out of the bedroom, he sees that Sandy Earl has beaten him to the door and is now standing there wearing nothing but his underpants with his pistol in his hand. Marcus walks over to the door and looks out to see who it is.

As they stand there looking out the open door, neither he nor Sandy Earl had to ask the question of why the person had knocked on their door with such urgency at such an early hour of the morning. The answer is as obvious as the noses on their faces and can be seen from miles and miles away. The warehouse that houses the cotton is on fire and is burning out of control.

"John Jr. wants every able-bodied man on the place over at the warehouse. Right now!" the man yells out as he runs to the next house and bangs on the door.

DeEtta comes into the front room to see what was going on. And as she steps into the room, she sees the glow from the fire glowing so bright that it gives the appearance that the whole world is ablaze. As she walks up to the door and looks out, she sees the flames reaching high into the night sky. She can also hear the distant echoes of voices as the men yell to one another while making ready to confront the raging inferno.

Sandy Earl and Marcus quickly get dressed and hop into Sandy Earl's truck and race off to the warehouse. As they pull up to the fire, they see John Jr. barking out conflicting orders like he had done back when the levee broke. A sense of panic and fear can be heard in his voice as the fire continues to intensify. Sandy Earl and Marcus quickly load several barrels onto the back of the truck and race off to the well to fill them with water only to find after getting there that the well closest to the warehouse is no longer operable.

After returning to the warehouse, they see that the two pump trucks from the firehouse in town have arrived and they are spraying whatever water they could carry onto the flames, which is the equivalent of pouring two buckets of water down the mouth of an erupting volcano. Steven, who has been fighting the fire tooth and nail, orders everyone to get back as the structure starts to collapse. John Jr. tries to contradict his orders but is silenced when a gush of flames shoots out from the building as the roof collapses and nearly sets him on fire.

With the glow from the blazing structure as a background, Steven and John Jr. stand staring at one another, their silhouettes producing a picture that in a lot of ways represents the true depth of the hatred that somehow has been allowed to fester within them toward one another.

By late afternoon the next day, the fire had all but burnt itself out. Steven, covered with soot, is sitting on the bumper of one of the fire trucks while his brother John Jr. is standing across from him. They both are having a conversation with the fire chief.

Sandy Earl and Marcus are only a few yards away sitting on Sandy Earl's truck's tailgate, looking out at the heap of still glowing cinders of what was once a warehouse full of cotton.

"I can tell you right now that this fire was intentionally set. And the person who did it didn't even try to hide it," the fire chief is heard saying.

"I wonder which one of these fucking niggers did it!" John Jr. shouts.

"What in the hell are you talking about?" Steven shouts back at him. "Please! Tell me just why in the hell would they burn down the only place within a twenty-mile radius that they can store their crops? Can you answer that for me, please?" Steven stands up and readies himself for a fight. "I can tell you who in the hell probably started it. And it's not any of these people standing here who have been working their asses off trying to put the damn thing out either!" Steven says as he references to the large group of sharecroppers who are also covered in soot from fighting the blaze. "Let's start with that pack of drunken degenerates that you've hired on here," Steven adds just prior to his brother rushing into him.

The brothers fight one another as if their only purpose is to end the life of the other. The fight goes on for several minutes before the older white warehouse employees restrain Steven and several of John Jr.'s friends do the same with him. And as the two groups stand before each other, it is obvious that there is no love to be shared from either side for the other.

The days following the fire are filled with conspiracy theories, finger-pointing, and unfounded accusations as the feud between the Shegogg brothers grows. The town and surrounding area eventually get drawn in as agitators fan the flames of hatred and distrust between the two sides. Even the sharecroppers can tell that this isn't going to end well for anyone, especially for them if it continues to escalate.

DeEtta and Marcus had started moving in with Sandy Earl shortly after Mary left for California. And they are still in the process of moving some of their things in while removing and giving away the stuff that Mary left behind that they or Sandy Earl don't want. While Sandy Earl and Marcus are loading some of Mary's old stuff onto the truck, DeEtta and Julia are in the house sorting out what goes and what stays.

After the truck is fully loaded, Marcus and Sandy Earl head off up the hill toward the other sharecroppers' houses to give the items away to whoever needs or wants them.

While they are gone, DeEtta asks Julia, "Can you keep a secret?"

Julia replies, "Yes, you know I can."

DeEtta then tells Julia while wearing a huge smile, "I think that I'm pregnant!"

While expecting her friend to dance for joy after hearing the news, DeEtta is somewhat shocked as Julia looks down at the floor with a long face.

"What's wrong?" DeEtta asks.

Julia replies, "So am I."

After getting over the initial shock, DeEtta takes Julia by the hand as they both sit down on the bed. Wanting so badly to ask Julia who the father is but realizing that there would be plenty of time in the future to have that discussion, she instead gives her friend what she really needs at the moment. And that is someone to hold on to and talk with.

After unloading the truck, Sandy Earl and Marcus return home to find Julia and DeEtta sitting out on the front porch.

"Being that you two are done, I guess that means we are as well?" Marcus says as he walks past them and into the house. Sandy Earl stops and tries to strike up a conversation. But neither DeEtta nor Julia seem to be in a talking mood. So he heads on into the house as well.

A few days after having the conversation with Julia, DeEtta eventually breaks the news of her pregnancy to Marcus. He is so elated that he practically tells anyone and everyone who will listen and even some that don't want to listen. The joys of parenthood are upon them.

DeEtta is extremely happy to be pregnant, but the happiness has a bittersweet taste to it. The sweet is that she and her husband Marcus have made something they can love and cherish forever. And the bitter is that, although she and her best friend share the same condition, the perception of their circumstances will be looked at through two different lenses.

A couple of weeks later, late one evening after Sandy Earl has returned from the fields and Marcus has gotten off work, the two of them and DeEtta sit in the front room with the doors and windows open, hoping to catch a soothing evening breeze. DeEtta stares out the window as the sun's rays generate a bright orange streak through a line of clouds that are stretched out across the distant sky.

"What are you thinking, sweetheart?" Marcus asks DeEtta.

"Oh, nothing much," DeEtta answers.

"You're thinking about something because for the last few days, you have been sitting around here humming church songs like your mama. And not saying two words to anyone about anything. Now, I know something is on your mind. Is the baby all right?" Marcus asks.

"The baby is fine! And you're right, there is something going on. But I promised Julia not to tell anyone," DeEtta answers.

"Excuse me," Sandy Earl says as he interrupts the conversation. "I can leave if there is something that you two need to discuss in private."

"Sit back down. You don't need to leave. Everyone is going to find out about it sooner or later anyway. But you need to promise not to tell anyone before then," DeEtta says. After Sandy Earl and Marcus both agree not to tell anyone. DeEtta says, "Julia is pregnant."

"I can't believe that she went and got herself pregnant by that white boy!" Sandy Earl says.

"How do you know that it's Steven's?" DeEtta asks as she comes to her friend's defense.

"Because she's always up in his face! Everybody sees it!" Sandy Earl says. "I saw her not too long ago. Up in their store, all grinning and smiling. I tried to tell her about herself then but she didn't want to hear it," Sandy Earl adds.

"Well, whoever the father may be, she's my friend. And I intend to be there for her just like she would be there for me if it was the other way around," DeEtta says as she starts to get emotional.

"She is our friend! And I think that we all should be there for her," Marcus says as he puts his arm around his wife and looks over at Sandy Earl as he is shaking his head from side to side.

"I agree! But I did try to tell her. And she didn't want to hear it!" Sandy Earl says while he walks over to the front door to look out at the sun just as it starts to disappear over the horizon.

DeEtta talks Marcus and Sandy Earl into letting Julia move in with them because she knows that once Julia's father finds out that she is with child, life for her there will become almost unbearable. And if what Sandy Earl said about Steven Shegogg being the father is true, she will surely be thrown out to fend for herself. The following Saturday, Marcus takes DeEtta to see Julia.

DeEtta knocks on the door while Marcus waits in the truck.

"What brings you by here so early in the morning?" Julia asks after opening the door and seeing that it is DeEtta.

"I've been worrying about my friend and wanted to see how she is doing," DeEtta replies.

Julia waves to Marcus as she steps out onto the porch and closes the door behind her. Her eyes immediately fill with tears as she thinks about how to respond.

And before she can figure out what she wants to say, DeEtta says, "I told Marcus and Sandy Earl about you being pregnant. And they both said that you can come and stay with us if you want to."

Julia first thought is *How could you have told someone when you promised not to?* But as reason sinks in, she realizes that it was such a heavy burden to have put on her in the first place, especially in her present condition. And that DeEtta is only trying to be a good friend and help.

"This is my problem and my mistake. And it's not fair to you guys for me to just take my problems and ruin your lives with them. I'm not sure what I'm going to do right now. But I don't think moving in with you is the answer. But thanks for the offer," Julia says before going back into the house and shutting the door behind her.

DeEtta stands there for a moment silently staring at the closed door as she tries to think of something to say that would change Julia's mind. Her first thoughts are, *"Maybe I shouldn't have told Marcus and Sandy Earl about the pregnancy. And maybe I should have just waited until she was ready to tell them in her own way."*

CHAPTER 22

One Truth

Late summer 1990—After sleeping through the night, Mama Dee is awakened by the sound of a squirrel scratching around in the flower pots on her balcony. As she slowly raises her head from the pillow, the squirrel looks at her through the glass of the French doors and starts to bark at her as if he is daring her to get up out of that bed and run him off like she had done countless times in the past.

While still weak from the treatments from the day before, Mama Dee reaches over and picks up a plastic cup partly filled with water from the nightstand. She then throws it against the glass. When the cup hits the glass, the squirrel jumps clean out of sight and knocks one of the small flower pots on the balcony's rail onto the floor.

Stefan and Clarice, who are just down the hall, hear the noise from the breaking flower pot and come rushing into Mama Dee's room. As they enter the room, they find Mama Dee lying in bed, laughing at how the squirrel had reacted when the cup hit the glass.

"Are you all right, Mama?" Stefan asks before realizing that she is laughing instead of crying.

"Yes, I'm fine," Mama Dee answers as she lays her head back down on the pillow.

After seeing the cup and water on the floor, Stefan asks, "Why are we throwing things? Is there something that we should know about?"

Mama Dee, while still laughing, starts to explain. But after seeing the serious looks on Stefan and Clarice's faces, she says, "Never mind. You had to have been here."

Clarice picks the cup up off the floor and says to Mama Dee, "I'm going to take this downstairs and bring you back something to eat. You've been sleeping for over ten hours, and I know that you must be starving."

While Clarice is gone, Stefan gets a towel from the bathroom to clean up the spilled water. After getting up the water, he sits down on the edge of the bed next to Mama Dee and asks her, "How are you feeling today?"

Mama Dee slowly sits up in the bed with the help of Stefan. After adjusting herself to try and get as comfortable as possible, she replies, "Better than yesterday."

"Sorry that I dozed off and didn't finish telling you about how you came to be who you are. But I was so tired," Mama Dee says.

Stefan replies, "I understand, Mama." Mama Dee then takes him by the hand and rubs it as she continues with the story from where she had left off.

* * *

The end of summer 1941—As the church choir rehearses for tomorrow's service. DeEtta and Julia, who have started to take more active roles in the church, both have individual solos that they are sometimes called upon to sing. Never knowing when one of them might get called upon, they do their best to never miss a rehearsal so that they are always prepared. Many of the older choir members who have been singing in the choir for years are often heard saying, "They must be heaven-sent because their voices are like hearing an angel calling you home."

Even Ms. Lillie has said more than once, "Their singing is as welcoming to the ears as the chirpings of the morning songbirds." And everyone knows that it is a given that whenever either one of them is called on to sing, their performance will most certainly bring the entire congregation to its feet.

Tomorrow is the pastor's twenty-fifth anniversary, and several of the surrounding churches have been invited to the celebration. So the choir wants to make sure that its big guns are ready for the occasion. DeEtta and Julia, while working together on something special for the event, agree that they should maybe start with something that they can do as a duet and then maybe later on in the program do a solo apiece to get the crowd going.

While rehearsing the duet portion of the program, they are interrupted by a loud banging at the church's front door. It's Sheriff Pickens and one of his deputies. They want to ask the people in the church some questions.

After the sheriff has a brief conversation with Rev. Mitchel, the reverend agrees to let him speak to the choir. After receiving a reminder from the reverend about where he is, Sheriff Perkins removes his hat as he walks to the front of the church. He then pulls a picture of a Black man in a prison uniform from a folder and circulates it among the twenty or so people in the church. As the photograph makes its way around, the sheriff asks, "Has anyone seen the man in the picture? He has been on the run from the law for three years. And a couple of days ago, we got word that he might be heading this way. He is wanted for killing a white man up in the state of Missouri. And if you see him, you best give us a call," the sheriff says.

As the picture reaches DeEtta and Julia, who are standing up front only a few yards down from where the sheriff is standing, they both start to get weak in the knees after seeing that the face on the picture is Marques. As the members talk among themselves, the sheriff and his deputy soon realize that either none of them know anything or that they know something and none of them are willing to say anything. So they gather up the photos that they had brought with them and leave.

Soon after the sheriff and deputy are gone, DeEtta and Julia quickly sing their songs and come up with an excuse for why they needed to leave too. DeEtta drives the truck home as fast as the road conditions will allow. After getting there, she and Julia rushed into the house to tell Marcus and Sandy Earl what the sheriff had told them. But, by then, the word had already gotten to them. And they were as shocked to hear it as anyone.

"Do you think that Marques really could have done something like that?" Julia asks.

"Some men only can take so much. And there is no telling what that man had done to him to make him kill him," Sandy Earl replies.

"Yea, I agree," says Marcus as he put his arm around DeEtta and pulls her close to him.

"I guess that's why he got the hell away from around here. Because God knows that some of these bastards down here most definitely deserve to be killed," Sandy Earl says as he recalls what had happened to his father that night some years back.

"I don't know why he did what he did, but I hope to God that they never catch him," Julia says.

The next morning, as they get ready for church, DeEtta looks in the mirror and notices that her stomach is starting to show from the baby that she is carrying inside. As she hums a song to her unborn child, she rubs her stomach and thinks about her mother Mary and wonders what she might be doing on a Sunday morning as beautiful as this. After she finishes getting dressed, she takes a pencil and a piece of paper from the dresser drawer and writes her mother a letter while Marcus and Sandy Earl are getting dressed.

She writes, *Hello, Mama, it's your daughter DeEtta. I hope this letter finds you doing well. I know that you have only been gone for a few months, but so much has happened since you left. The first and most important thing is that I have some fantastic news to tell you. Marcus and I are having a baby! I wish so much that you can be here when it comes, but I know that California is so far away and that it costs so much to make such a journey.*

Sandy Earl and Marcus are doing well, and Marcus and I did move in with Sandy Earl. We all miss you so much and hope that someday we will all be able to get together if only for a little while. Mrs. Loo is still as friendly as ever and she often ask about you whenever we go into her store.

The church members took a collection for you. They collected a love offering of seven dollars and some change for you, which I have included in the envelope. They all send their love.

The other thing that happened is, the cotton warehouse burned to the ground. And while it burned, the two Shegogg boys got into a fight and tried to kill one another. Seems like the whole town is now divided. Either you are with John Jr., or you are with Steven.

Since it's a white folk mess, most of us have been able to keep clear of it so far. Well, I'll let you go for now, and we are hoping for a letter back soon. Love, DeEtta.

After noticing that there was no noise coming from the bedroom, Marcuse knocks on the door and asks, "Are you okay in there, honey?"

DeEtta replies, "Yes! Just writing Mama a letter. Are you guys ready to leave?"

Sandy Earl and Marcus both answer at the same time, "Yes."

While they are driving to church, DeEtta gives the letter to Marcus and asks him to take it to the post office for her on Monday. Marcus sticks the letter in the glove box as they pull up to the church. They can tell right off from the number of cars that are lining the street that the church is going to be packed full. Julia is standing outside, waiting on DeEtta. She wants to see if their outfits match for when they do their duet together.

During most of the program, and especially when DeEtta and Julia sing the songs that they had rehearsed, the entire church is on its feet, shouting praise and singing along. Rev. Mitchel even cries a couple of times as the choir is singing.

And as he speaks, he proclaims, "This is a day that my wife and I will remember for the rest of our days."

After the service is over and the people are walking to their cars and wagons, everyone stops as they pass the choir to congratulate them on the great job that they had done. Rev. Mitchel and his wife personally thank DeEtta and Julia. It had been truly a great day for all who attended.

While driving home, Marcus says, "Today, while we were in church, I heard that John Jr. is looking for some laborers to help with rebuilding the warehouse."

"I don't think that there are many Black people around here who would want to work for him, not directly anyway," Sandy Earl replies.

"They said that he is willing to pay a dollar a day. With the baby coming and all, I'm thinking about working with him on the weekends," Marcus says.

"I don't know about that," Sandy Earl says. "I personally would be afraid of not getting paid. Now, if Steven was doing it, that would be altogether different."

As they pull up to the house, they see Julia standing out front. DeEtta can tell that something is wrong from the look on her face.

"Didn't we just see you at church a little while ago?" Sandy Earl jokingly says as he gets out of Marcus's car.

Julia doesn't reply, she just looks down at the ground so that Sandy Earl can't see that she has been crying. DeEtta hops out the car and goes over to her. DeEtta then takes her by the hand and takes her in the house.

And while Marcus and Sandy Earl wait outside, DeEtta and Julia talk.

"What's going on?" DeEtta asks.

"My mother walked into the room this morning while I was getting dressed and saw my stomach. She then asked me the obvious question, 'Are you pregnant?' And after having a lengthy conversation with her, she told me that I either had to find a way to get rid of it or tell my father. So I told him on the way home from church, and he stopped the truck and told me to get out. And as he was driving off he said, let them know once I've found somewhere else to live so that he can drop off my things. I got no place else to go," Julia says as she breaks down and starts to sob. "And the funny thing about it is, I can't really blame him. He and my mother are already taking care of me, my sister, and my little brother in that two-room shack. If we squeezed another person in there, one of the walls would probably fall down," Julia adds as she tries to make light of her situation while attempting to pull herself together. "I can't kill my baby, DeEtta," Julia says.

"And I won't let you. You are staying here with us, and I'm not taking no for an answer. I'll have Marcus and Sandy Earl go and get your things," DeEtta replies as she gives Julia a hug.

It doesn't take long for the word about Julia being pregnant to spread through the gossip mill. And it is no surprise that it eventually reaches the ears of Kathy May Shegogg.

"Son! What in the hell were you thinking when you got that nigger girl pregnant?" Mrs. Shegogg asks Steven.

"What do you mean got somebody pregnant? Who in the hell told you that? John?" Steven says.

"Boy, don't lie to me! Everybody in the whole damn town been talking about how you and that Martin girl, Julia, been hanging out together. I've even seen it for myself with my own damn eyes from the balcony out there," Kathy May says as she gets up and closes her bedroom door after seeing that Ms. Lillie is cleaning down the hall.

Kathy May's questioning catches Steven by surprise and his initial response is to defend Julia. "Okay, if it makes you happy Mama, yes, it's my baby! What do you want from me? An apology for soiling the Shegogg's good name? But you know what? I think it's little too late for me to have soiled the name because my daddy and y'all beloved John Jr. has already beat me to it," Steven says just before Kathy May slaps him across the face.

"Your daddy did everything for us. Why do you think that we have all this? And I will be damned if I let his own flesh and blood talk like that about him!" Kathy May says.

"All of what Mama? You have been locked up in this here room for the last fifteen years. And why? Is it because you didn't want to come to terms with all of the affairs that he has had with other women over the years? Or was it because he was just a mean, heartless person who didn't care about anything unless it carried his name?" Steven says as he storms out the door and slams it behind him. He then gets in his car and goes to find Julia.

"Good afternoon, Mr. Martin," Steven says to Julia's father as he drives up. Julia's father is sitting on his front porch, chewing on a plug of tobacco. He acts as if he doesn't even see Steven. Steven then gets out of his car and walks up to the porch. Julia's father spits on the ground as Steven walks up. Steven can tell from the look in Mr. Martin's eyes that if he thought that he could get away with it, he would probably shoot him dead where he stands.

"Is Julia here?" Steven asks.

"Julia doesn't live here anymore. And at this point, I don't know or even care where she is at," Mr. Martin says before spitting on the ground once more and getting up and going into the house.

Steven walks back to his car and starts to get in when he hears someone standing on the side of the house say, "She is at the Wells' place." As he looks over at where the voice is coming from, he sees Julia's sister hiding on the side of the house. Steven thanks her and then drives off.

Before making it to DeEtta's house, he sees DeEtta and Julia walking down the road on their way back from the green fields. Each of them carries a bundle of greens, which they have just finished picking and are planning on cooking them for Sandy Earl and Marcus's dinner that evening.

DeEtta notices Steven's car as it is coming down the hill toward them. "Look who's coming," she says to Julia as Steven pulls the car over and gets out.

Steven then walks up to Julia and says, "We need to talk."

"Yeah, we do," Julia replies as she hands her bundle of greens to DeEtta.

"Do I need to wait here for you?" DeEtta asks as she looks at Steven as if he has somehow betrayed the trust that they had in him.

"No, you can go. I'll be all right," Julia says. She and Steven then walk toward the old wagon trail as they talk.

"So when were you going to tell me?" Steven asks.

"I've wanted to tell you each and every time that I saw you. But it never seemed to come out of my mouth," Julia replies.

"You do know that a lot of people around here, my mother being one of them, think that it's my baby that you are carrying," Steven says.

"I've heard that too. And I corrected them each and every time someone says it. But you know as well as I do that the truth never makes for good gossip," Julia replies.

"Seeing that everyone is insisting that it is my child that you are carrying, can you at least tell me who the father is?" Steven asks.

"I can but you won't know him. His name is Marques," Julia answers.

"You know, I would have given everything for that to have been my child that you are carrying," Steven says.

"You are one special person," Julia says as she and Steven embrace. DeEtta looks back just as they hug one another and shakes her head before continuing on to the house.

Steven jokingly says to Julia as they walk back to his car, "You know what! If I were you, I would let them think that it's my baby that you are carrying. That way, won't anybody around here give you any shit. Because nobody in their right mind would dare harm anything with the Shegogg name on it. And another thing, I would love to see the look on my mother's face when she sees that the baby isn't mixed."

Julia smiles and replies, "Like I said, "You are special."

She then continues walking up the road toward the house.

CHAPTER 23

The Last Harvest Fest

Late Summer 1990—"It sure is good to see you up and about this morning, Mama," Stefan says as he walks out onto the balcony and sits down beside Mama Dee.

"It feels good to be out of that bed," Mama Dee replies while looking out over the morning mist that covers the valley below. "What do you all have planned for today?" Mama Dee asks.

"Nothing this morning, but later on today, that estate lawyer is coming by. He's bringing the last of the papers that I need to sign for the rest of the Shegogg estate. Apparently, she still owned the two lots of land that the old store and bank sat on," Stefan says as he stands up and looks out over the railing.

"It sure is a pretty morning," Mama Dee says before getting up and going back inside the house. After looking out over the railing for a moment or so longer, Stefan follows her on inside.

Mama Dee sits down on the bed, and Stefan sets in the chair next to the balcony door and continues to look out as he says to her, "The kids will be starting school soon. We enrolled them into that private school over near Grenada, and from looking at the literature that they gave us, I don't think that there are a lot of Black kids that go there. I sure hope Jamil and Jazmin like it."

"Private school, huh? I remember, back when I was their age, we had only one school that we could go to. And it was inside of the church that we went to. Our church served as a church on Sundays and a school for us kids during the week. Rev. Mitchel's wife was the only teacher. She taught grades one through eight all in the same room," Mama Dee recalls. "These kids sure are blessed," she adds as she lies back against the pillows and stretches out on the bed. "You know…I made it all the way through the eighth grade. And would have gone farther if we had had a school to go to," she says.

"Your father and Uncle Sandy Earl only made it through the third grade. It wasn't because of them not wanting to continue to go or not being smart enough! It was because back then, Black boys were expected to start work at a very young age. And by the time your uncle was fourteen, he was picking more than a hundred pounds of cotton a day by himself," she explains.

"You know, it's sad when you think about it. Back when we were slaves or would work for almost nothing, we were called hard workers. Now that we want to be paid for what we do, we all of a sudden get labeled as being lazy," Mama Dee says with a chuckle.

Stefan looks over at her and shakes his head and smiles while looking at his pager, only partly listening to what she is saying. After looking at his pager for the third time, Stefan says to Mama Dee, "I'll be back up to check on you later. I need to go and make a few work calls." And before leaving, he kisses her on the forehead.

No sooner than Stefan walks out the door, Jazmin walks in carrying a tray of food. "Good morning, Mama Dee!" Jazmin says as she sets the tray down on the nightstand next to the bed. "I sure hope that you're hungry because Mama told me to stay up here with you until you eat. So unless you are ready to spend your entire morning with me, I suggest that you go ahead and get your grub on, sister. That way, both of us can get on with enjoying the rest of our day," Jazmin adds while looking at Mama Dee and smiling.

Mama Dee looks over at the tray food and smiles back at Jazmin. Jazmin removes the cover from the plate and helps Mama Dee to sit up in the bed. After eating a small portion of the food, Mama Dee asks Jazmin to move the tray and come sit next to her on the bed so that they can talk.

"So are you dating yet?" Mama Dee asks, knowing that the question would not only cause Jazmin to blush but also shift the conversation away from her not eating.

Jazmin laughs as she answers, "Yes, ma'am."

"Well! Aren't you going to tell me about him?" Mama Dee asks.

After she stops laughing, Jazmin answers, "His name is Kevin, and he lives back in Detroit."

"Oh, one of those long-distance relationships, huh?" Mama Dee asks. "Those are usually the tuff ones to make work," Mama Dee adds. After taking another sip of her orange juice, Mama Dee asks, "Are you planning on getting married someday? And I don't necessarily mean soon or even to this Kevin fella. I'm talking about your long-range plans, like after you get out of college."

Jazmin blushes once more before answering. "Yes, I suppose so, someday," she says.

"Do you want to have any children?" Mama Dee asks as she hands the empty juice glass to Jazmin to sit on the nightstand.

Jazmin quickly answers that particular question, as if she had previously given it some thought, "Yes, ma'am. A boy and a girl."

Mama Dee lays her head back against her pillow and says, "I always wanted kids too. Sonny and I were planning on having as many as the Lord would have allowed. But I guess it just wasn't meant to be."

Jazmin sees that Mama Dee is getting tired, so she collects the dishes and turns out the light before leaving the room. As Mama Dee lays there with her eyes partly closed, the room is illuminated only by the light of day coming through the windows of French doors. Her mind takes her back to another particular time in her past.

* * *

Early Fall 1941—"DeEtta, do you feel like walking to town with me?" Julia asks after making out a list of items that she and DeEtta agreed to make for this year's Harvest Fest celebration.

DeEtta laughs and says, "Sure, the walk will probably do both of us some good," making reference to both of their bellies sticking out due to their pregnancy.

While they are walking along, Julia asks DeEtta, "Did you hear about someone shooting the window out of the Shegogg's store?"

DeEtta replies, "Yes, Marcus was telling me about it. He said that he heard some of the white guys over at the gin talking about it. They were saying that John Jr. had one of his friends do it. Something about John Jr. being jealous because he's not making any money since the warehouse burned down, and Steven not giving him any of the money that the store's making."

"That doesn't surprise me one bit. Hell, if John Jr. would have kept his promise and paid the guys like he had said that he would, he would have had a new building built by now. Instead, all he got is a pile of lumber sitting over there rotting," Julia says with a snicker.

"I know! He still owes Marcus twenty dollars that I know that we'll never see one penny of. And the Lord knows that we need our money," DeEtta replies.

As they continue to walk, they come to the place on the old wagon path where the Shegogg mansion can be seen off in the far distance. Kathy May Shegogg is sitting out on her balcony like she often does.

"Don't look now, but I think that Mrs. Shegogg is looking at us," DeEtta says while trying not to let on that they know that they are being watched. While thinking about the conversation that she and Steven had a while back, Julia looks directly at her and waves.

They can tell right away that she wasn't expecting it because shortly after being waved at, Kathy May throws both of her hands into the air and goes back inside.

"I'm not sure that that was a smart thing you did back there," DeEtta says to Julia. Especially being that you are carrying her son's baby," DeEtta adds.

"What do you mean carrying her son's baby?" Julia replies as she stops walking.

"I thought when I saw you two hugging that day, that it must have been his baby. That was why I never asked," DeEtta explains.

"No! This is not Steven's baby that I'm carrying! Steven is a very nice person and all. But do you actually think that I would lay down and open myself up for someone whose family has done so many horrible things to all the people I love and care about?" Julia asks.

"Being that you put it like that, the answer is no. And I'm sorry for assuming and not asking…So do you accept my apology?" DeEtta asks.

"I guess so," Julia replies.

"Okay, now that we got that out of the way, who is the daddy?" DeEtta asks.

"You have to promise not to tell anyone. Including Marcus and Sandy Earl," Julia says as she references the inclusions to the last secret that she told DeEtta.

"This time, I really promise," DeEtta says.

"It's Marques's baby," Julia says as she starts back to walking. After taking a second or so to process what Julia has just told her, DeEtta continues walking as well. Neither of them says another word for the remainder of the walk to town.

After making it to town, DeEtta goes to the post office to check and see if there is any mail. At the same time, Julia heads over to the Shegogg's store to start shopping for the items that they need for the Harvest Fest. As soon as Julia walks into the store, she sees Steven working in his office with the door open.

After seeing her, Steven waves and then signals for her to come over to his office. Julia walks in the direction of his office. She encounters two older white women who have, without a doubt, heard the rumors about a Black woman being pregnant with Steven's baby.

The two women give Julia a look that would lead one to believe that she isn't fit to draw breath. But by now, Julia has grown used to the menacing looks and whispers of impurity. So after observing their stares, she simply avoids further eye contact as she continues to walk toward Steven's office.

Once inside, Steven closes the door. "So how are we doing today?" He asks in a very upbeat fashion as he tries to project that he has gotten past Julia being pregnant by someone other than himself.

"We're doing just fine," Julia replies as she plops down in the chair that's sitting directly in front of the small rotating fan that he has in his office.

"Don't tell me you walked all the way to town?" Steven asks.

"Okay, I won't tell you that DeEtta and I walked all the way to town," Julia replies. She then leans her head back in an attempt to take in as much of the breeze being generated by the tiny fan as physically possible.

"I bet that was a sight to see. You two with your bellies all sticking out wobbling down the road," Steve jokingly says as he gives Julia a cup of water from the water cooler that is sitting in the corner in his office.

"Thanks! You sure know the way to a woman's heart," Julia says as she drinks down the cup of water.

As DeEtta walks into the post office, she sees that the lines are long. And after waiting for a while with little or no movement, she decides to do the shopping first and then come back to check on the mail. As she gets ready to leave, the clerk from behind the counter who knows that she has been looking for a letter from her mother calls out to her. "DeEtta! Don't leave just yet. You got a letter."

DeEtta's face lights up like an electric light bulb as she races over to get it. After getting the letter, DeEtta walks out of the post office and sits down on the bench out front and opens it. The letter reads, *My dear DeEtta, I hope that my letter finds you, Sandy Earl, and Marcus doing well. I was so happy to hear that you are going to have a baby that I danced and paced around the house for half the night. This must indeed be a precious time in you and Marcus's lives.*

It brought to mind when I was pregnant with you guys. At first, Sonny and I didn't have much of anything except for each other. Then, when you two came, it all of a sudden felt like we had a whole lot.

This here California is something else! I have never seen anything like it. You know, back when I was a kid, I always wondered why we colored water blue when we drew pictures. Now I know why! The Pacific Ocean is as blue as anything that I have ever seen before. And when I look out over it, my heart feels the presence of Sonny, Sandy Earl, and you. Continue to stay strong, and I will always keep y'all in my prayers. Love, Mama.

After reading the letter, DeEtta sits on the bench for a bit longer while she silently sends multiple thanks up to the heavens above for allowing her to hear back from her mother. She then heads over to the Shegogg's store to help Julia with the shopping. When she walks into the store, she sees Julia standing over by the shopping carts talking with one of the cashiers.

"Did you get anything in the mail?" Julia asks as they get a cart and start to push it.

"Yes, I did. And it's from Mama," DeEtta says with a smile on her face.

"What did she say?" Julia asks.

"She wished us all well and talked about how beautiful California is," DeEtta replies.

Once they are done with their shopping, DeEtta and Julia head for home. While walking down the path, DeEtta pulls out the letter from her mother and shows it to Julia. Julia takes the letter and reads it aloud. After reading it, she gives it back to DeEtta.

As DeEtta is sticking the letter back into her pocket, Julia asks her, "Do you think that we'll ever be able to go to places like California?"

"Sure, someday," DeEtta answers.

"It would be so wonderful to take off my shoes and just run barefoot along the edge of the Pacific Ocean… Especially if the water is as blue as your mother says it is," Julia says as she reflects on what is written in the letter.

As they come to about the halfway point, DeEtta says to Julia, "I need to stop and rest for a little bit." After finding a nice shady spot under a tree, they both sit down on the ground. Julia notices that DeEtta is sweating really bad and holding her stomach as if she is in pain.

"Are you all right?" Julia asks.

After some hesitation and rocking back and forth, DeEtta replies, "No, not really." She falls back and rolls over onto her side.

As Julia jumps to her feet, she can see that DeEtta is bleeding. "Oh my God!" Julia says. "DeEtta! You stay right here! I'm going to get some help! *Don't you die on me now!*" Julia says as she takes off in the direction toward town.

About forty-five minutes later, Julia returns with Steven. DeEtta is still lying there on the ground, barely alive. They quickly load her into Steven's car and rush her off to the hospital. About an hour after Julia, Steven, and DeEtta reach the hospital, Marcus and Sandy Earl arrive to find that DeEtta is still in surgery.

"What happened?" Marcus asks Julia after seeing her and Steven sitting in the waiting room.

With her eyes red from crying, Julia rushes over to Marcus and starts to explain what happened. But before she can finish explaining, she is interrupted by the doctor when he walks into the waiting room. After Marcus introduces himself as DeEtta's husband, the doctor asks him to step out into the hallway so that they can talk in private.

The doctor tells Marcus that the good news is that DeEtta is stable and that she will recover. But there is also some bad news. And the bad news is that the baby was lost and that DeEtta will not be able to have any more children. Marcus falls back against the wall and starts to weep like a child as he slides down into the floor and balls up. After hearing him crying, Julia and Sandy Earls run out into the hall and puts their arms around him.

Steven watches from the waiting room's doorway while wishing that there was something that he could do to ease Marcus's pain.

After going home, DeEtta pretty much stays in her bedroom during the next few weeks, not talking to anyone or eating much at all.

"Honey, we need to try and pull out of this," Marcus says as he sits down on the bed next to her after coming home after work. DeEtta looks over at him and acknowledges that he said something but doesn't say anything in reply.

Marcus then takes her by the hand and pulls her in close to him. He then says to her, "You know, it feels like the day we lost our baby, I lost my wife too."

DeEtta looks up into his eyes and says, "I know, but it just hurts inside so much." She then puts both her arms around him, and they cry themselves to sleep.

Ever since Irma Jean found out what had happened to DeEtta, she starts stopping by the house every day to do whatever is needed to help her feel better. On this particular day, Irma Jean feels that flowers are what is needed to cheer DeEtta up. So early that morning before the break of day, she sneaks into Kathy May Shegogg's flower garden and cuts and picks every flower that hasn't wilted from the cool night air that she could carry.

That morning when DeEtta comes out of her room, it looks like someone has robbed the town florist and hidden all of the stolen merchandise in their front room. Even after DeEtta comes out of her room, Irma Jean is still bringing in bunches of fresh-cut mums. It is one of the funniest things that DeEtta has ever seen, especially after Irma Jean tells her where she got the flowers from.

With the help of Irma Jean and her dear friend Julia, who stays at DeEtta's bedside almost each and every day while Marcus and Sandy Earl go to work, DeEtta slowly gets to what is to be her new normal after the loss of the baby.

"Look who is up and dressed," Marcus says as DeEtta comes out of their bedroom. "Why don't you take a ride to town with me?" he asks as he puts down the armful of firewood that he just brought into the house.

"I don't know about that," DeEtta replies.

"Oh, come on, it's Monday. And you haven't been anywhere in almost two months," Marcus says as he tries to encourage her to come with him.

"Well, okay," DeEtta reluctantly says.

As they pull onto Jefferson Davis street, they notice that the people who are out on the street are all crowded around the storefronts as if they are having meetings or something. Marcus pulls the car over and parks it in front of Mr. and Mrs. Loo's store. After he and DeEtta get out of the car, they walk across the street to the Shegogg's store. As they walk up to the door, they can see that everyone is listening quietly to what is being said on the radio.

The voice on the radio was that of the president United States, and he is saying that the Japanese have attacked the naval bases in Hawaii and the country is now at war.

CHAPTER 24

Life's Alteration

Early Fall 1990—"Mama Dee, have you ever been to a different country?" Jazmin asks, brushing Mama Dee's hair while she sits in her rocking chair on the balcony.

"Yes. Your grandfather and I went on several cruises. As a matter of fact, your mom and dad sent us on one the year before your grandfather died," Mama Dee replies.

"If you could go back to any of the places that you have been before, which place would you go back to?" Jazmin asks.

"It would probably be the island of St. Kitts. That's the island that has all of the charming little monkeys on it. And also because that is where your grandfather and I went for our belated honeymoon," Mama Dee answers.

"Belated honeymoon?" Jazmin asks.

"Yes, belated. You see, when your grandfather and I got married, we barely had enough money to make it through the winters. And as far as we knew, things like going on honeymoons to exotic places were something that only rich folks could afford to do back then," Mama Dee replies.

"So how long was it before you and grandpa finally got to go on one?" Jazmin asks.

"It was around our thirtieth wedding anniversary, and your grandfather surprised me with a cruise. And man, did we have a good time! The tiny little cabin that we stayed in on the ship even kind of reminded us of the shack we used to live in when we lived here," Mama Dee says as she reminisces.

"You two must have really loved one another because if my husband told me that I had to wait thirty years before going on our honeymoon, I would say, '*next*'!" Jazmin says as she and Mama Dee laugh.

"I would have waited a hundred years for a honeymoon if I had to for your grandfather. I guess they don't make men like him anymore," Mama Dee replies.

"You're right, Mama Dee. They don't make men like him anymore," Jazmin replies as she continues to brush Mama Dee's hair.

"Hey there, Mama Dee!" Jamil says as he walks into the room with the cordless phone in his hand.

"Good afternoon Jamil! And what brings you up here?" Mama Dee asks after seeing the phone in his hand.

"Mama told me to bring you the phone. I think it's Uncle Sandy Earl," Jamil answers.

Mama Dee's face lights up with a huge smile as she takes the phone from Jamil.

Just as Mama Dee and Sandy Earl start to talk, Jazmin and Jamil, as they both are getting ready to leave the room, ask Mama Dee, "Tell Uncle Sandy Earl hello!"

Mama Dee stops them, gives them the phone, and says, "Tell him yourself!" After briefly speaking with their great uncle, they give the phone back to Mama Dee and walk out of the room, closing the door behind them.

Once Mama Dee and Sandy Earl start talking about old times, who has died, and who is still living, it is like they can't stop talking. They talk nonstop for almost two hours. And once they are done talking about the old days, they start talking about their grandchildren. Sandy Earl even talks about his great-grandchildren.

Before they are done talking, Mama Dee tells him about when she received the phone call from Irma Jean and that Irma Jean had stopped by her house in Detroit to see her, but they had already moved to the house here in Mississippi. Irma Jean and her family were doing well.

As the conversation starts to slow to almost a trickle, DeEtta tells her brother how much she loves him and misses the days when seeing his face was a daily pleasure that she truly regrets no longer having.

Sandy Earl then tells DeEtta that she is and will always be not only on his mind but also in his heart. And as Mama Dee hangs up the phone, she recalls the last time that she and her brother, Sandy Earl, were together and the tiny little shack that they once called home.

* * *

Early Winter 1941—"I don't see why you want to go and do a fool thing like that," DeEtta says to Sandy Earl after he tells her that he has enlisted into the army.

"DeEtta! They attacked us, for heaven's sake!" Sandy Earl replies.

"No! They attacked *them*. And *them* are the same people that won't let you sit down in a restaurant next to *them* and eat a *damn* meal. *Them* are the same people who will lynch you if you forget your place. *They* are who disfigured our father, if you can remember!" DeEtta says.

"DeEtta, if we ever want to be a significant part of this here country, we need to do our part. Even if it means going off to fight and maybe dying for it," Sandy Earl says.

"You want to *die*? You don't need to go halfway around the world to do that! Just go find John Jr. and his drunk ass friends and tell them to go to hell. I'm pretty damn sure that they would kill you right on the spot. And not do a day in jail for doing it!" DeEtta says as she goes into her bedroom and slams the door shut.

Sandy Earl looks over at Marcus in hopes of some understanding. Marcus looks at him and shakes his head as to say, "Man, that's between you and your sister." Sandy Earl then goes outside and gets into a waiting car with some of his friends who have enlisted as well. The car then drives off.

Marcus goes into the bedroom where DeEtta is lying across the bed, upset.

"Don't you come in here trying to take up for him either!" DeEtta says to Marcus without looking up at him.

"I wasn't going to take up for him. But he is your brother, and I know as well as you do that y'all love one another. And neither one of y'all would want them words that I heard coming out of your mouths to be the last word you two say to one another until he gets back. So if I were you, I would go and find my brother and tell him how much I love him. And how much I'm going to miss him before it's too late," Marcus replies.

DeEtta thinks about what Marcus has said for only a little while before coming to the conclusion that he is right and if something were to happen to Sandy Earl while he was away, she would never forgive herself. "Okay, you are right," DeEtta tells Marcus before getting the keys to the car and going out to try and find him before he leaves.

As DeEtta is driving through the center of town, she sees a huge crowd gathered in front of the Loo's store. Some of the men are wearing white robes and carrying torches. "Get out here, you chink motherfuckers!" one of them yells out as he throws a rock through the large front display windows. DeEtta slows the car down but doesn't stop as she turns onto the Shegogg store lot. She then parks the car in a spot where she cannot be seen.

While sitting in the car, watching what is unfolding, she sees the bus loaded with the Negro enlistees drive past. All of their faces are glued to the window of the bus as it drives through the crowed street past the men wearing their white hoods and carrying the lit torches. DeEtta's heart flutters with grief as the prospect of her never seeing Sandy Earl again becomes real. Moments later, the bus taillights vanish into the night.

As DeEtta continues to sit in her car, she notices something about one of the men wearing the white robes. He is the one doing most of the talking. It is something about the way that he walks and stands that strikes her attention. And as she listens carefully to his voice, she knows for sure who it is. It is John Jr., and as she continues to look and listen, she realizes that the other men who are wearing hoods are his friends. And as they continue to shout out for the Loos to come out, the more convinced she becomes.

After the cries for the Loos to come out and face a lynching goes unanswered, one of the robed men yells out, "*Burn their asses out of there, John!*" And with that, the man who is doing most of the talking heaves one of the flaming torches through the broken window.

In almost nothing flat, the fire ignites the rolls of cloth and sewing materials used in the front display and quickly spreads throughout the store. And within minutes, the entire place turns into a raging inferno. DeEtta can hardly believe what she is witnessing.

It is as frightening a thing to see as what she had witnessed happen to her father many years ago when she was a little girl. And she now feels as she felt back then: *I should do something to help.* But the reality is the same, and there is nothing that she can do.

Being too afraid to help or even drive off, DeEtta sits in her car and watches as the building burns. Soon, the roof of the structure starts to crumbles down into the flames as the crowd begins to disperse. As DeEtta starts the car to drive off, she reflects on how no one comes to the Loo's aid, not the sheriff, nor fire department, not even a friend attempted to come to their aid.

"Hey, DeEtta!" a voice calls out from the side door of the Shegogg store. DeEtta looks over to where the sound is coming from and sees Steven standing in the doorway. Steven waves his arm as he beckons for her to come over to the door. Before getting out of the car, DeEtta looks around to sees if any of the men wearing the white robes are still standing around. By then, they all have gone down the street and are now standing across the street from the sheriff's office drinking beer with some of the deputies.

As DeEtta gets out of her car, Steven calls out, "Bring your car over here!" DeEtta, somewhat puzzled as to why he is asking her to bring her car over, starts it and drives over near the door. As Steven opens the back door of the building wider, she sees Mr. and Mrs. Loo. They are trembling with fear, but they are not injured. DeEtta feels a huge feeling of relief as she looks into their terrified eyes .

Steven opens the back door of the car, and Mr. and Mrs. Loo quickly slip into the car, and DeEtta drives off. After making it home, DeEtta parks the car at the side of the house and sneaks the Loos inside. At first, Marcus is somewhat surprised to see that DeEtta has brought home some guests. But the feeling of surprise is short-lived once DeEtta tells him about what happened.

While DeEtta is fixing the Loos something to eat, Marcus asks, "Were you able to catch your brother before his bus pulled out?"

DeEtta replies, "No," as she continues to prepare the meal.

After a while, Mrs. Loo starts to come out of the shock of losing their home, their store, and everything in them and begins to speak. "Thank you!" she says to DeEtta while holding her hand.

DeEtta smiles at Mrs. Loo as she softly says, "You are welcome."

For the next few weeks, Marcus, DeEtta, and Julia hid the Loo family out at their house. This continues until Marcus can get in touch with Mr. Loo's brother, who lives in the Detroit area. After some discussion, Marcus and DeEtta agree to take them to him.

As Marcus, DeEtta, and the Loos leave early in the morning heading for Detroit, they anticipate being gone for three days. So Julia asks Irma Jean to come and stay with her while they are away.

Even though the trip is risky, DeEtta is really excited about going. They all know that if they are pulled over by the police and the police see that the car has Negros and Orientals in it—even though the Loos are Chinese, not Japanese—there is no telling how they will react, especially while they are below the Mason-Dixie line.

Even though DeEtta and Marcus have never been outside of the state of Mississippi but once in their life and that was to take Jimmy to see his father who was in the hospital in Memphis, a chance to finally see some of the things that they had so often heard Marques talk about makes them all the more prepared to take the risk. And as they drive past the sign that reads, "Welcome to Arkansas," Marcus says to DeEtta, "We are now out of Mississippi!"

After crossing the state line, to DeEtta, the air that she breathed in seems to somehow taste different. The sky that she looked at seemed to somehow look clearer. And she most definitely felt somehow freer. Although the state of Arkansas's track record with Jim Crow was the mirror image of Mississippi's, DeEtta and her family had not had to endure it.

While Marcus, DeEtta, and the Loos are heading north to Detroit, Julia spends the evening helping Irma Jean with her homework.

"So, why did DeEtta and Marcus go to Detroit?" Irma Jean asks.

"They had to take a friend." Julia answers.

"Who?" Irma Jean asks.

Knowing that it is best if no one knows that the Loos had been hiding out at their house, not even Irma Jean, who was as loyal to DeEtta as anyone could be, Julia answers, "It's some grown folks' mess. And you really don't want or need to know. Can you accept that as an answer for now?" Julia says.

"I suppose so." Irma, Jean replies.

The following night after Irma Jean has gone to bed, Julia sits next to the fireplace reading a book. There is a knock at the door. Julia places her book face down on the small table next to the chair that she is sitting in and gets up and answer it.

To her surprise, it is Steven. "How are you doing?" Steven asks.

"I'm okay…what brings you out this time of night?" Julia asks.

"Marcus told me that they were taking the Loos to Detroit, and I figured that you would be here by yourself. So I stopped by to check on you to make sure that you are okay," Steven explains. "I told them that if they ran into any problems while driving, they could call me for help. That is, if they needed to," Steven adds as Julia steps out the door and closes it behind her so that the sound of their voices doesn't wake up Irma Jean.

After a moment of silence, Steven says, "Actually! There is another reason I stopped by, other than to check on you and see if you needed anything. And…it is to let you know that I have enlisted into navy and will be leaving in a few days," Steven says.

"Why are you joining the navy? I mean, you have it all. A thriving business, a large house to live in. And probably more money than you can spend," Julia says as they both sit down on the steps of the porch.

"That thing about having it all isn't what it's all cracked up to be, you know. It seems like I been looking for a way out of this life as long as I can remember. Who knows? Maybe this here war is what I need to finally make it happen," Steven says as he leans his head back and looks up at the numerous stars that are sprinkled across a night sky's pitch-black canvas.

"I wish that I could say that I know what you mean, but being that I been poor my whole life, I really can't say that. Now, can I?" Julia says with a chuckle.

Steven replies, "I know! It's hard given the way things are for a person of color to feel sorry for the rich white boy. But I guess what I'm trying to say is, you, DeEtta, and Marcus are going to be something in life. And it might not be rich or live in a big fancy house. But it will be what you decided for it to be. Not a prewritten script like my life has been.

"Hell! I'm the son of Big John, for all its good as well as all its bad. And that is something that I will never be able to live up to or outlive. My father…most people hated or feared him. Very few respected him. Especially the ones who would hang around and smile and grin in his face all the time. Not one person that came to his funeral said, 'They are going to miss him.' Not a one!"

"I guess I kind of see what you are talking about," Julia says as she put her arm around his waist.

And as they continue with their conversation, the cool winter air slowly surrounds them, and the steam from their breath starts to appear as they sit and talk into the earliest of the morning hour. Steven then asks Julia to tell his friends Marcus and DeEtta bye for him and to also tell them that they all will always hold a special place in his heart. He then walks off into the early morning mist as he heads home.

After driving through the night and well into the following day, Marcus, DeEtta, and the Loos finally make it to the house of Mr. Loo's brother. Knowing how long Marcus had been driving, Mr. Loo's sister-in-law insists on Marcus and DeEtta spending the night with them before making the long journey back home. She then takes them to the spare bedroom on the second floor of the house and tells them, "This is where you will be sleeping, and I won't take no for an answer."

As they walk into the room, Marcus and DeEtta don't let on, but they are stunned, not only by the size of the room but the size of the bed as well. They have never seen or, heaven knows, slept in a place so large or beautiful before in their lives.

After getting probably one of the best nights of sleep that either of them has had in a long time, they are awakened by the smell of coffee and bacon cooking down in the kitchen. After bathing in a real bathtub with running hot and cold water, DeEtta feels as if she must have died and gone to heaven.

After breakfast, DeEtta and Marcus load their things into the car as they get ready to leave. Mr. and Mrs. Loo walk out to their car with them.

And as they are about to get into the car, Mrs. Loo says to them, "We can never thank you enough for what you have done for us. And if you ever need anything, please don't be afraid to ask." Mr. Loo shakes his head in agreement. Mr. Loo's brother then have the four of them pose for a couple of photographs. And as the Loo family waves goodbye, Marcus and DeEtta head back to Mississippi.

While driving home, DeEtta can't stop talking about how big and beautiful Mr. Loo's brother's house is and how large and soft the bed was. And at that moment while reliving what they had experienced, both of them realize that they have somehow, in this short period of time, outgrown Mississippi and the Jim Crow laws that it uses that kept them from prospering. And that they need to find a way out.

The closer they get to the Mississippi state line, the more they feel like they don't want to return. It is as if they had learned to fly, and then all of a sudden, someone tells them, "Give me them wings! Flying is not for you."

But Marcus knows that they have to return because everything they had ever worked for and owned was there, including his job at the co-op. Yet, deep in their hearts lay the truth, and that truth is if they returned, it would be twice as hard, if not impossible, to ever leave again, even though it would be in their best interest to do so.

After they reenter the state of Mississippi, the conversation diminishes into a deep state of reflection about the possibilities of if they had not returned. While he reflects, Marcus sees himself slowly sliding down the same slope that his father and his father's father had as they relinquished the possibility of hoping for a better life and settled for one of just being satisfied that they were able to get in another full day of hard work before the sun told them to stop by taking away the light.

DeEtta pictures herself as being forty years older and living in the same little shack that her father took his last breath in with no children to nurture or care for. There is only Marcus to cling to when the storms of life come raging down on them. She then puts her warm hand atop his as it rests on the seat of the car and starts to hum one of her mother's favorite song as they drive on into the night.

As they pull the car up in front of their house in the late hour of the night, the house is dark and quiet. DeEtta asks Marcus, "Would it be okay if we sit here for a while?"

Marcus, not being quite ready either to step back into their reality just yet, lays his head back and replies in a soft low voice, "Sure, sweetheart."

The next morning, Julia and Irma Jean are up early as they make breakfast for Marcus, DeEtta, and themselves. Julia tells Marcus and DeEtta about Steven joining the navy and what he had said about keeping them in his heart.

"We sure are going to miss him around here," DeEtta says.

"I guess that means that John Jr. will be running everything now," Marcus adds as he shakes his head in disbelief.

"You mean running everything into the ground, don't you?" DeEtta says while having a hard time believing it as well.

A few weeks later, Marcus and DeEtta go to town to do their Saturday morning shopping like they have done almost every Saturday morning since Mary moved to California. While driving through town, they see one of the white cashiers who works at the Shegogg store. She is standing at the stop sign down the street from the store, waiting to cross the street.

"Hi, there!" the cashier says as she steps off the sidewalk and walks up to the car as if she wants to talk about something.

Marcus and DeEtta think that it is somewhat strange that they have known her for more than ten years from working in the store, and she has never said more than a couple of words to them.

"Good morning!" DeEtta says as the woman walks up to the window of the car.

"What can we do for you?" Marcus adds as he tries to figure out what could she possibly have to say to them.

"Hi there, my name is June. But y'all probably already knows that from coming into the Shegogg's store all of the time," June says with a slight grin. She then continues by saying, "The reason I stopped y'all is to let you all know that there is a new store that just opened down on

Magnolia street. And they have everything that you could imagine on their shelves.

"As a matter of fact, that's where I work now. So y'all come on by and see me sometime. Okay?" she concludes.

DeEtta replies, "We just might do that sometime."

Marcus nods his head while still wondering why she approached them about going to a different store when she knows right and well that they stay on the Shegogg's place.

After the somewhat strange encounter, Marcus and DeEtta continue on their way. After reaching the Shegogg's store, Marcus parks the car across the street in front of the burned out building that was once the Chinamen store. Each and every time that they see the structure, he and DeEtta can't help but wonder how are the Loos doing now that they are living up in Detroit.

Before getting out of the car, they both sit there for a moment. It is as if they are waiting for Mrs. Loo to come walking out of the door of their store wearing her usual smile and saying, "Good morning." But as they look across the street, they see a couple of John Jr's friends sitting on the lot of the Shegogg's store. And just the sight of them brings Marcus and DeEtta back to the reality of the real world and evaporates any momentary pleasant thoughts that they might have had.

DeEtta and Marcus get out of their car and cross the street. As they walk into the store, they can tell right away that the place is no longer being managed by Steven. The shelves are practically empty, and the items that would normally be on them are sitting in front of them, still in the boxes that they were shipped in. There are only two cashiers, and they both look to be new.

After walking through the disorganized and partly empty store, DeEtta and Marcus make their way to exit without buying a single item. After getting back in their car, they decide to take a look at the new store that the lady had told them about. And as they pull up in front of the building, it is obvious what is happening. The once coveted Shegogg empire is now under siege and all of the respect, fear, financial and political clout that it embodied is now crumbling.

With Big John dead and Steven off fighting in the war, it leaves only John Jr. and Mrs. Shegogg to run things. Mrs. Shegogg has no idea about how to do it. John Jr. is someone who has a reputation of not paying anyone, except for the person at the counter of the local liquor store.

John Jr.'s inability to pay people, along with his explosive temper, makes it easy for the new competitor to get a foothold. And before long, all of his store employees quit and come to work at the new grocery store chain owned by the New York businessman, Mr. Baum.

CHAPTER 25

The How

Early Fall 1990—After hearing the doorbell ring, Jazmin and Jamil races for the door. Jamil gets there first, but Jazmin is not far behind. Jamil opens the door and sees that there is a medium height, somewhat overweight white gentleman standing on the other side.

"Hi there, my name is Jeff Little. Is your father home? I think that he's expecting me," the gentleman says as he removes his sunglasses.

Just as Mr. Little finishes introducing himself, Stefan comes down the steps and walks over to the door. "Hi, there. I'm Stefan Waters. We talked over the phone. Come on in," Stefan says as he shows Jeff Little the way to the library. After going into the library, Stefan closes the door.

"Have a seat," Stefan says while extending his arm out toward the chair facing his desk. Jeff sits down in the chair, and Stefan sits down at his desk across from him. Stefan then asks him if he could explain in greater detail some of the things they talked about over the phone.

And as Jeff starts to speak, Clarice comes into the library and sits down next to her husband. Stefan introduces Clarice to Mr. Little.

"Please call me, Jeff," he replies before continuing with what he was about to say. "Like I said over the phone when we talked a few months ago, Kathy May Shegogg spelled out very specifically who she wanted to leave everything to. And that was, and is, the firstborn child of your mother, who was Julia Ann Martin? Am I correct?" Jeff asks.

"Yes, I am her first and only born child," Stefan acknowledges.

"We had just about given up on trying to find you until a man over at the supermarket told us about his great aunt. He said she knew everything about everybody that lived on the Shegogg place back then. That is the most talkative old lady that I have ever met. Hard to believe that she was one hundred four years old at the time when we talked. The people in the old folk's home called her Ms. Lillie, I believe.

"Anyway, from what we got from her, and what is written in Mrs. Shegogg's Bible, we were able to find DeEtta Wells. I tell you another thing, that lady Mrs. Shegogg must have had a lot to pray about because she sure wrote in her Bible a lot. She even wrote down the exact day that your mama and her friend DeEtta left to go to Detroit. It seemed like it kind of hurt her heart when she found out that they had left, from what she wrote in her Bible.

"After putting everything together, I was able to get you certified as the last living relative. That's why I could send you the keys to the house and the bank account information on what little money she had left. All I need now is for you to sign the last of these papers, and I'll be on my way. Oh, I have some boxes of stuff that belonged to Mrs. Shegogg in the car that I need to give you," Jeff says while Stefan is signing the papers.

Stefan and Jamil then follow him out to his car to retrieve the boxes containing Kathy May Shegogg's belongings. "Take these and put them in the library so that your mother and I can go through them later while I go upstairs and check on Mama," Stefan tells Jamil.

After walking into her bedroom, Stefan stands over Mama Dee and looks down at her as he whispers a soft prayer. Assuming that she is asleep, he then whispers to himself as he sits down in the chair next to her bed, "Mama, why won't you tell me what happened to her?"

Mama Dee slowly opens her eyes as she hears his voice. She then tries to raise her hand to rub his cheek as she starts to speak but is too weak. She realizes and understands that the pain of what happened on that rainy day back in the spring of 1942 is something that she can no longer shield him from. She then tells him the story of how she came to be the person that he calls mother.

* * *

Spring 1942—"Did you hear about Mrs. Monroe's boy?" Ms. Lillie asks her friend while they are sitting in their usual spot before the start of Sunday service in the pew in front of Marcus, Julia, and DeEtta.

"No, I didn't," her friend replies.

"Well…Sallie Davison is now doing the cleaning at the Monroe's house. And she told me that the Western

Union man came to their house yesterday with a telegram for Mr. and Mrs. Monroe."

"Mrs. Monroe answered the door. And after seeing
that it was a Western Union telegram, she assumed
that it was something that maybe one of their relatives
had sent. You know, a special message or something
because her birthday is only a few days away. So she
called Mr. Monroe and the other kids into the front room
before she opened it. And as a matter of fact, she let little
Missy open it. Child! The note was from the Department
of the Navy. And it was informing them that their son
Mark had been killed in the war! I can't believe that
they would send something like that through Western
Union," Ms. Lillie tells her friend.

DeEtta and Julia try to act as if they are not listening
to the conversation. But the thought of receiving a special
telegram telling you that your loved one has been killed
in the war makes the war and its deadly consequences
feel all the nearer.

"Did she happen to say what ship he was on?" Julia
asks Ms. Lillie as she interrupts their conversation.

"No! She didn't!" Ms. Lillie answers as she rolls her
eyes at Julia, who is now in the eighth month of her
pregnancy. Julia begins to worry, knowing from the last
letter that she received from Steven that some of the guys
from the area who joined around the same time that he
did were assigned to the same ship that he is on.

Steven, who had only been gone for a little more than
four months, had written Julia almost every week since
he left, except for the last two. Julia, on the other hand,
had only written to him twice. Her lack of writing him

was not something that she chose to do; it was because she had to sneak and mail the letter from the post office in Granada where his name wasn't as well known.

Now DeEtta had just received a letter from Sandy Earl, who was still in Georgia waiting to be deployed to Europe. But according to him, the deployment was still probably a couple of months away. But no one in his regiment knew for sure because the army only told you things on a need-to-know basis, he wrote in his letter.

After the church service is over, Julia tells DeEtta and Marcus that she has something that she needs to take care of and that she would find a ride home after she is done doing what she needs to do. After watching DeEtta and Marcus drive off, Julia takes off walking toward the old trail that goes past the Shegogg's house.

While she is walking, Julia tries to figure out how or even should she ask Mrs. Shegogg about Steven. And before long, she finds herself standing at the Shegogg's back door, knowing that if she continued to think about it, she would eventually convince herself not to follow through. So, without hesitation, she knocks on the door and waits for someone to answer.

Knowing that Sundays are the day that Mrs. Shegogg usually gives the help the day off, Julia hopes that she would maybe have the opportunity to talk to her alone. That way, she can ask about Steven and let her know that all of the rumors that are going around about her unborn baby belonging to Steven are simply not true. After waiting for several long minutes without anyone answering, Julia decides to leave and head on home.

While Julia is walking across the yard toward the wagon trail, John Jr. pulls into the driveway and sees her just as she steps off into the woods. Still drunk from the night before, he calls for his mother as he storms into the house. Julia, not knowing that John Jr. saw her, continues her trek down the trail.

While walking down the trail, Julia gets an eerie feeling that she is being watched. And as she turns and looks up toward the house, she sees Mrs. Shegogg standing on her balcony, looking down at her. Julia stops and stares back at her. And it is as if they both know that they need to talk, but they both are afraid to hear what the other one might have to say.

"*Momma*! Where are you!" John Jr. slurs as he staggers into his mother's bedroom.

"What the hell do you want?" Kathy May asks as she walks in from the balcony with a piece a paper in her hand.

"What did you and Julia talk about?" John Jr. asks as he uses the wall to prop himself up so that he doesn't fall flat on his face.

"None of your damn business! *And get the hell out of my house! You're drunk again*!" Kathy May shouts.

"If that nigger bitch thinks that she and that mixed baby of Steven's is going to get one fucking dime of Daddy's money, I will see them both in hell first!" John Jr. swears.

Kathy May looks at her son for a moment before speaking and wonders, *How could I have given birth to someone like this?*

She then says as she wipes a tear from her face, "You are just like your father in some ways, and in other ways, you are not. The only thing that you give a damn about is what or who you can control and the hell with what everyone else around you want or needs to make their lives worth living. And in that way, you are like your father. But you are lazy, and you are stupid, and he wasn't. And in that way, you are not.

"You been drunk for so long and done slept with so many diseased infested women that you couldn't give me a grandchild if you wanted to. Could you?" Kathy May says as she sits down on the bed, laying the piece of paper that she had in her hand down beside her.

"I could make a baby if I wanted to. And it wouldn't be with one of them darkies either like your precious little Steven went and done," John Jr. replies.

Kathy May looks at John Jr. and says, "Don't you ever let me hear my son Steven's name come out of your mouth again! Steven was the only thing good that came out of me and your father's marriage. Now get the hell out of my house!" Kathy May says. And as she stands to her feet, the piece of paper falls onto the floor.

John Jr. sees the piece of paper on the floor and picks it up and reads it. The words on it read, *It is with our deepest regret that we inform you that your son Steven Shegogg was kill…*

"*Get the hell out of my house!*" Kathy May shouts as she hits John Jr. across the chest and face with her fists while crying.

John Jr. staggers down the steps and out onto the front porch. As he looks out at the horizon, he sees several dark rain clouds coming in their direction. And the wind starts to blow.

He then wobbles over to his car and reaches in through an open window. After retrieving a bottle of whiskey from the front seat, he opens it and turns it up. And while he stands there drinking from his bottle, the rain starts to fall.

As the droplets of rain start to pelt Julia about the head and shoulders, she veers off the path and makes her way to the main road, hoping that she will see someone she knows who can give her a ride home. Once on the road, the rain and the wind pick up considerably. And as a blinding rain starts to fall, Julia flags down the first car that she sees, hoping that they will stop and give her a ride. As the car gets closer, she not only recognizes it, but she realizes who is driving it.

Back at DeEtta's house, Marcus is working on his car.

"Damn, I'm glad I got that starter changed before it started pouring down. This is one of those rains that's going to last all night," Marcus says as he pulls off his wet coat and lays it across the chair next to the fireplace. "You're awful quiet over there. What're you doing?" he asks DeEtta.

"Making some booties for my friend's baby," DeEtta replies.

"Speaking of Julia, shouldn't she be home by now?" Marcus asks.

"I was just thinking the same thing," DeEtta replies.

"I think that I'm going to take a drive up the hill and see who it is that's bringing her home. You want to ride with me?" Marcus asks.

After driving up the hill, Marcus sees one of the other church members sitting on his front porch, watching the rain as it falls.

"Hi there," Marcus yells out from the open car window.

"Hi there, Marcus," the gentlemen replies.

"Have you seen Julia?" Marcus asks.

"Not since after church," the man says. His wife then walks out the door and adds, "She was walking up toward the old wagon trail when I last saw her."

Marcus tells them thanks, and he and DeEtta turn the car around and head toward the trail. DeEtta can't help but think about what had happened to her the last time that she and Julia had walked the path together, but she doesn't tell Marcus what she is thinking because all that would do is make him as nervous as she is. By the time they make it to the trail, the heavy rain has already saturated the soil so much that they cannot drive the car down it.

"Well! Why don't you take the car and drive down the main road to where the trail ends? I'll walk the trail, and you can pick me up on the other end," Marcus says while putting on his hat and coat. As Marcus opens the car door, a strong wind tries to blow it out of his hand as he steps out into the raging storm. DeEtta quickly slides across the seat to the steering wheel and turns the car around and heads toward the main road.

The darkening of the day caused by the rain clouds is eventually replaced with the darkness of night as DeEtta sits waiting at the roadside near the exit end of the trail. After about an hour and a half wait, Marcus emerges from the trail without Julia. Marcus, soaking wet from head to toe, climbs into the passenger side of the car.

"Where should we look next?" DeEtta asks as Marcus takes the wet hat off of his head.

"Let's turn around and go back to the house, maybe she's there by now," Marcus says.

DeEtta quickly turns the car around. And as she is driving back down the road toward the house. They see Julia stagger out of the woods and fall onto the shoulder of the road. DeEtta slams on the brakes, and they both jump out of the car and run over to her.

Julia has been beaten so severely that she is hardly breathing. Her eyes are swollen shut, and she is bleeding profusely. Marcus picks her up and climbs into the back seat of the car with her, he can see that she has gone into labor.

"DeEtta drive to the hospital!" Marcus shouts.

As they are racing down the road toward town, Marcus asks Julia, "Who done this to you?"

Julia whispers, "John Jr.," before passing away. As the lightning flashes and the thunder rumbles, the amount of falling rain increases by the second.

As DeEtta looks back at her friends still body, the child makes its way from her womb. And as she turns her head back to look at the road, she almost loses control as she comes to a curve. While trying to regain control of the car, she sees a person standing in the middle of the road. It is too late to hit the brakes or steer around them. The car slams directly into the person, knocking him into the ditch.

After bringing the car to a stop, DeEtta and Marcus look through the rear window. It doesn't take long for them to recognize who the car sitting on the side of the road belongs to. Realizing that it was probably John Jr they had hit and knowing what he had done to Julia and what the local authorities' reaction would be if they took her to the hospital in town and tried to explain what had happened, Marcus and DeEtta instead make the decision to take Julia's body and her newborn baby to the hospital in Memphis.

The next morning as the heavy rains continue to fall, several police cars are sitting in the drive of the Shegogg's house. The sheriff is upstairs with Kathy May while two of his deputies are standing on the front porch. "I am so sorry for your grief, Mrs. Shegogg, but with that levee breaking like it did last night, he probably never saw the water coming while he was trying to change that flat tire. And I promise you that as soon as it stops raining, we will drag that creek and see if we can find anything," the sheriff says as he walks toward the steps. "One other thing, Mrs. Shegogg, where do you want us to put his car?" the sheriff asks.

"Put it in the barn over by the stables," Kathy May replies as she sits down on the edge of her bed.

"That woman sure has been through a lot. Can you imagine losing both of the children in the same week?" the sheriff says to his deputies as they walk out the door.

"Lillie May! Can you come in here and talk with me for a little bit?" Kathy May asks.

"Yes, ma'am, Mrs. Shegogg, I'll be right there as soon as I'm done with this here floor," Ms. Lillie replies.

"That floor can wait. I need to ask you something," Kathy May insists.

Ms. Lillie walks into Kathy May's bedroom.

"Come on in and have a seat over here next to me," Kathy May says. After Ms. Lillie sits down, Kathy May asks her, "I know good and well that if anything happens on this here place, including inside of this house, you know about it. Having said that, I need to ask you something, and I really need you to tell me the truth."

"Sure, anything for you, Mrs. Shegogg," Ms. Lillie replies.

"Is that baby in Julia Ann's belly the child of my dead son Steven?" Kathy May asks while looking Ms. Lillie in her eyes. Ms. Lillie starts to tremble and perspire as she struggles to answer the question.

But by her reaction, Kathy May can tell what the answer to the question is without Ms. Lillie even saying a word. And without saying another word, Kathy May Shegogg stretches out facedown across her bed. Ms. Lillie slowly gets up and leaves the room.

* * *

1990—As the last truck carrying their furniture drives through the gate, Stefan looks at Clarice and displays a fake smile to try and hide his sadness.

Clarice puts her arm around his waist and says, "Mama Dee and Julia would have wanted it this way. Don't you think?" Stefan nods his head in agreement.

He then closes the front gate and looks over at the "For Sale" sign before getting in the car and heading back to where they belong—Detroit.

THE END

MAMA DEE

Written by Earl Lynn

I t is a story about the strength of family, the love for friends, and the path that life sometimes forces you to take. DeEtta, the daughter of a Black Mississippi sharecropper, learns to endure the continuously daunting pressures brought on by the systemic Jim Crow laws as she matures into a woman during the pre-civil rights era.

As an older woman, she is forced to recall her past when she is brought back to the place where it all transpired. Her memories will make you smile, laugh, and maybe even cry.

CPSIA information can be obtained
at www.ICGtesting.com
Printed in the USA
LVHW070747140623
749653LV00010B/1373